Vi

KIM THÚY

Vi

Translated from the French by SHEILA FISCHMAN

Vintage Canada

VINTAGE CANADA EDITION, 2019

Published by Vintage Canada, a division of Penguin Random House Canada
Limited, in 2019. Originally published in hardcover by Random House
Canada, a division of Penguin Random House Canada Limited, in 2018.
Distributed in Canada by Penguin Random House Canada Limited, Toronto.

www.penguinrandomhouse.ca

Library and Archives Canada Cataloguing in Publication

Thúy, Kim
[Vi. English]
    Vi / Kim Thúy ; [translated by] Sheila Fischman.

Translation of: Vi.

ISBN 978-0-7352-7280-4
eBook ISBN 978-0-7352-7281-1

    I. Fischman, Sheila, translator II. Title. III. Title: Vi. English.

PS8639.H89V513 2019   C843'.6   C2017-905123-7

Book design by CS Richardson

Cover image © Paul Bucknall / Arcangel Images

Interior images from *The Illustrated Book of Canaries and Cage-Birds,
British and Foreign*, Cassell & Co., London, 1877. Illustration by William
Rutledge. © mmello / Getty Images

Printed and bound in the United States of America

2 4 6 8 9 7 5 3 1

Penguin
Random House
VINTAGE CANADA

I WAS EIGHT YEARS OLD when our house was plunged into silence.

Under the fan fixed to the ivory wall of the dining room, a large bright-red sheet of rigid cardboard held a block of three hundred and sixty-five sheets of paper. On each was marked the month, the day of the week, and two dates: one according to the solar calendar, the other according to the lunar calendar. As soon as I was able to climb onto a chair, the task of tearing off a page was reserved for me when I woke up. I was the guardian of time. That privilege was taken away from me when my older brothers, Long and Lộc, turned seventeen. Beginning on that birthday, which we didn't celebrate, my mother cried every morning in front of the calendar. It seemed to me that she was being torn apart each time she ripped off that day's page. The tick-tock of the clock that usually put us to sleep at afternoon nap time suddenly sounded like a bomb waiting to explode.

I was the baby of the family, the only sister of my three big brothers, the one everyone protected like precious bottles of perfume behind glassed-in doors. Even though my young age meant I was somewhat sheltered from my family's concerns, I knew that the two older boys would have to leave for the battlefield on the day they turned eighteen. Whether they were sent to Cambodia to fight Pol Pot or to the frontier with China, both destinations reserved for them the same fate, the same death.

MY PATERNAL GRANDFATHER had graduated from the Faculty of Law at the Université de Hanoi, where he was identified as "indigenous." France took charge of educating its subjects but did not accord the same value to diplomas awarded in its colonies. It may have been right to do so because the realities of life in Indochina had nothing in common with those of France. On the other hand, course requirements and exam questions were the same. My grandfather often told us that after the written examinations came a series of orals that led to the baccalaureate. For the French course, he'd had to translate in front of his teachers a Vietnamese poem into French and another in the opposite direction. Mathematics problems also had to be solved orally. The final test was to contend with the hostility of those who would decide on his future while still keeping his composure.

The teachers' intransigence didn't surprise the students because, in the social hierarchy, intellectuals occupied the top of the pyramid. They sat there as wise men and would be addressed as *"Professeur"* by their students all their lives. It was unthinkable to question what they said because they possessed the universal truth. That is why my grandfather had never protested when his teachers gave him a French name. From lack of knowledge or as an act of resistance, his parents had not done so. In his classes, then, from year to year, from one professor to another, he

would acquire a new name. Henri Lê Văn An.
Philippe Lê Văn An. Pascal Lê Văn An . . . Of all these
names, he ended up retaining Antoine and transformed
Lê Văn An into a family name.

BACK IN SAIGON, diploma in hand, my paternal grandfather became a respected judge and a fabulously wealthy landowner. He expressed his pride at having created at the same time an empire and an enviable reputation by giving his own name to each of his children: Thérèse Lê Văn An. Jeanne Lê Văn An. Marie Lê Văn An . . . and my father, Jean Lê Văn An. In contrast to me, my father was the only boy in a family of six girls. Like me, my father arrived last, just as everyone had stopped hoping for a standard-bearer. His birth transformed the life of my grandmother who, until then, had suffered every day from mean-spirited remarks about her inability to beget an heir. She had been torn between her own desire to be her husband's only wife and his duty to choose a second spouse. Luckily for her, her husband was one of those who had adopted the French practice of monogamy. Or perhaps he was quite simply in love with my grandmother, a woman known throughout Cochin-China for her graceful beauty and her delight in the pleasures of the senses.

MY PATERNAL GRANDMOTHER first met my grand-father very early one morning at the floating market in Cái Bè, a district on one of the arms of the Mekong that was half land, half water. Every day since 1732, merchants had been bringing their crops of fruits and vegetables to that part of the delta to sell to wholesalers. From far away the colour of the wood, mingled with the muddy brown of the water, gives the impression that melons, pineapples, pomelos, cabbages, gourds are floating independently of the men who have been waiting on the wharf since dawn to snap them up at the first opportunity. To this day, they transfer the fruits and vegetables by hand, as if these crops were entrusted to them, not sold. My grandmother was standing on the deck of the ferry, hypnotized by these repetitive and synchronized movements, when my grandfather noticed her. He was at first dazzled by the sun, then astounded by the young girl with her gener-ous curves accented by the folds of the Vietnamese dress that tolerates no superfluous movement and, above all, no indelicacy of intention. Snap fasteners down the right side keep the dress closed but never really fasten it. As a result, a single broad or abrupt movement causes the tunic to open all the way. For this reason, schoolgirls have to wear a camisole underneath to avoid accidental indecency. On the other hand, nothing can prevent the two long panels of the dress from replying to the breath of the wind and capturing hearts that find it hard to resist the power of beauty.

My grandfather fell into that trap. Blinded by the gentle, intermittent movement of the wings of the dress, he declared to his colleague that he would not leave Cái Bè without that woman. He first had to humiliate another young girl who'd been promised to him and cause offence to the elders in his family before he could touch the hands of my grandmother. Some believed that he was in love with her long-lashed almond eyes, others, with her fleshy lips, while still others were convinced that he'd been seduced by her full hips. No one had noticed the slender fingers holding a notebook against her bosom except my grandfather, who went on describing them for decades. He continued to evoke them long after age had transformed those smooth, tapering fingers into a fabulous myth or, at the very most, a lovers' tale.

BIÊN HÒA'S INDIGENOUS ARTS SCHOOL was at the height of its renown when my grandparents visited it to buy the seventh piece of ceramic for their seventh child; they were hesitating between the blue-flecked copper and the celadon glaze when my grandmother's waters broke. After pushing a few times, she gave birth to my father. Miraculously, my grandfather, two weeks earlier than predicted, was presented with a boy. His only boy.

My father was carried in my grandmother's fairy-like hands. And also in the hands of his six older sisters. And in those of the twenty-six nurses, cooks, maids, not counting those of the six hundred women who received adoringly in their open arms his well-formed face, his broad shoulders, his athlete's legs, and his seductive smile.

He could have studied sciences or the law like his sisters. But the affection of some and the love of others drew him away from his books and in so doing atrophied the gland that stimulates desire. How to desire when all is fulfilled in advance? Before he had even opened his eyes, the nipple of a lukewarm bottle of milk would be brushing his lips—up to the age of five or six. No one dared wake him for school, because his mother forbade anyone to interrupt his dreams. His nurse escorted him to his school desk, where she learned to read at the same time as he did. During his piano lessons, the maids fought over who could cool the back of his neck and freshen the ambient air with the sandalwood fan. He charmed his teacher simply by accompanying her warm-up notes with his voice. The more years passed, the larger the assembly in front of his house to hear the melodies he invented on the spot, without having the least aspiration to immortalize the slightest thing. The effort wearied him, as did the hands that kept dabbing at the drops of sweat on his nose. Still, he dared not refuse any of those attentions because, for him, to receive meant to give of oneself.

And so my father grew up in rapture, and also in a weightless void. He did not count his time in hours, but rather in the number of moves in a game of Chinese checkers, or the number of punishments his mother inflicted on the maids who let drop a bowl or a broom during his naps, or the number of love letters slipped anonymously into the letter box.

The fruits of the Lê Văn An empire would have easily permitted him to live on the margins of society. Fortunately, life loves to constantly alter the order of things, thus giving everyone the opportunity to follow its progress, to live within it. My father was barely twenty when agrarian reform divided in two the revenue and properties of the Lê Văn An empire. For the first time, farm workers were able to own the fields they ploughed. Just as these new policies were being implemented, my grandfather suffered a heart attack that diminished him by half. Without those shocks, my father would probably never have married my mother.

THE GIRLS OF ĐÀ LẠT were known for their pale complexions and their pink cheeks. Some believe that the high, cool plateaus safeguard their radiance, while others attribute the softness of their gestures to the mist that covers those valleys. My mother was an exception to this rule. Very quickly, very early, she accepted the fact that the boys would never say, "You are my springtime," even though her first name, Xuân, meant "spring," and she lived in a place called "the city of eternal spring." My mother had not inherited my grandmother's fine, smooth skin. Rather, she bore her father's Khmer genes, evident in her sturdy face, to which was added the ravages of acne throughout her adolescence. In order to turn away the eyes of others and to stitch the lips of sour mouths, she chose to become a woman who was fierce, armed with a will of iron and a hard, masculine vocabulary. She had come first in her class, from kindergarten right up to her final year at school. Without waiting to begin her studies in management, at a very young age she took over the reins of the family orchid farm, diversifying and reorganizing the production and transforming it into a business that grew exponentially.

She asked her father, a highly placed bureaucrat, if she could make improvements to the villa they rented out to vacationers. Very soon, she persuaded him to buy several other villas in order to meet the high demand: there were many people who sought a destination that reminded them of Europe, far from the daily and often stifling reality of tropical temperatures and conflicted relations between the dominant and the dominated. It was said that Đà Lạt, as its name indicated, had the power to provide pleasure for some and cool air for others.

My mother was fifteen years old when my father rented the Đà Lạt villa for the first time. My father didn't notice her because, when he passed by, she had to lower her eyes in order not to betray herself. She had spied on him from a distance during this initial visit of Judge Lê Văn An's family. The following year, and from then on, she insisted on taking part in meal preparation, overseeing every detail, from the carrots delicately carved into flowers and added to sauces, to the pieces of watermelon from which the seeds had been removed one by one with a toothpick so as not to disturb the flesh.

In the morning, the coffee had to be prepared from civet droppings, to which was attributed its caramelized taste, free of bitterness. My mother brought the morning coffee herself to my father on the terrace, hoping to see him applying brilliantine to his comb in order to shape his ebony hair, in the manner of Clark Gable. She had to catch her breath every time she saw him twist the comb, using the handle's pointed end to let fall a small S-shaped lock onto his brow. Even if she was standing just a few steps away, waiting for the coffee to seep, drop by drop, through the filter posed directly on one of the family's four rare Baccarat

glasses, she remained invisible to his eyes. She prolonged the pleasure of being in his company by
squeezing the filter's base, thus slowing the hot water's
progress through the layer of tightly packed coffee.
When it came to the last drops, she passed the back of
the spoon under the filter, an act that halted the flow.
Like all Vietnamese, my father took his coffee sweet-
ened with condensed milk, except for the first sip,
which he preferred black, pure. It was after this first
sip that he at last spoke to my mother.

ASTOUNDED BY THE UNUSUAL, velvety taste of the coffee, he turned his eyes in my mother's direction. She revealed to him the secret, showing him a small, misshapen ball dotted with seeds, gathered nearby from the plantations at Buôn Mê Thuột. Those balls came from wild civets that excreted the seeds whole after having eaten and digested ripe coffee cherries. And since the coolies did not have the right to avail themselves of the fruit they gathered for the owners, they had processed that excrement, which revealed itself to be more delicate, and above all rarer, than the regular harvest. My father became an instant convert. My mother volunteered to be his provider, and the one who schooled him in the aromas added piecemeal during the roasting, including the precious butter imported from France. Every two weeks, she carefully wrapped up a bag of coffee that she or an employee placed directly in my father's hands. She continued to observe this ritual during the rainy season, during the demonstrations in the Saigon streets, between the arrival of the Soviets in the North and the deployment of American soldiers in the South.

When the Lê Văn An family came to Đà Lạt, my mother continued to attend to the needs of my father, from coffee at dawn to the mosquito netting tucked in between the mattress and the bed. After my paternal grandfather's heart attack, my mother's parents invited him and his family to come more often, because the air of Đà Lạt was recognized for its healing powers.

Little by little, one of the villas became the residence of my father's family, even if they didn't have the means to pay for such a prolonged stay. My mother was delighted to see my father leaving his footprints on the earthen paths in the rose garden, and to hear his voice resonate among the pines at night.

The reforms and political changes had seriously impoverished the Lê Văn An family. Despite his carefree manner, my father was concerned about the erosion of his comfort. The deafening echo of the luxurious shell being drained from inside presented him with the image of a handsome prince with no kingdom. The fear of becoming a man in decline prompted him to take hold of my mother's hand in full flight. A single word escaped from his mouth: "Xuân." A single word from my father was enough to elicit an eternal vow from my mother: "Yes, I'll take care of everything."

GRAND LAC
HỒ XUÂN
HƯƠNG
~
lake of the
scent of spring

MY PARENTS' MARRIAGE was the event of the season at Đà Lạt. In order to satisfy the curiosity of the employees and residents of the town, my parents paraded in a convertible around Lake Hồ Xuân Hương before arriving at the reception, where the region's personages and dignitaries awaited them, and where all the women laid bets on my mother's unhappy future. On my father's arm, accompanied by her parents and her parents-in-law, my mother welcomed the guests at every table. My father and my two grandfathers thanked each group for their good wishes, toasting and emptying their glasses along with the table's spokesman. While the men cheated by filling their glasses with tea instead of whisky so they could complete their tour without falling down, my mother took pleasure in staring down the women who had openly called her a "monkey," "savage," and "transvestite" since her birth. To the ends of their lives, they continued to be mystified by my father's decision. My mother could make light of those insults, because from now on she would walk wrapped in the aura of my father's beauty.

To be my father's wife was to erase her flattened nostrils, her drooping eyelids, her square chin. She presented herself to people as Madame Lê Văn An, and demanded to be addressed as such by her employees, because each time this name was uttered, she heard my father whispering that her hair cascaded like the water of the Prenn Falls, that her pupils were as round and bright as two longan pits, and, above all, that no other woman understood him better than she did. From the first year of their marriage, she created a throne that allowed my father to be the monarch of his kingdom, by buying a warehouse and a villa in Saigon. He became the master of this depot where merchants and buyers came to submit their orders to a staff hired by my mother and officially overseen by my father. My mother advised their employees that he had to attend a number of social functions in the evening. Therefore it was strictly forbidden to disturb him in the morning, at noon, during his siestas, or when he was reflecting. All questions were to be addressed to her first, while all the decisions taken by my father were to be given priority in their execution.

SHE ARRIVED AT THE OFFICE at four thirty in the morning, after the wholesalers' market, to receive the first sales report from her employees. At seven o'clock she was back at the house, a few streets away. Those two properties would not have been accessible to her had she not mentioned her Chinese ancestors. Chợ Lớn was, and still is, the preserve of the Chinese community, known for its solidarity and its commercial might. Gontran de Poncins, a French viscount who was an author, adventurer, and journalist, had chosen to live there in 1955, in order to write a study of Chinese culture. Monsieur de Poncins suspected that the ancestral customs were better preserved in the colonies than in the mother country, or, at the very least, for a longer period. My grandfather Lê Văn An had long conversations on that subject with Monsieur de Poncins, and also concerning Monsieur Yvon Petra, born in Chợ Lớn, and who, in 1946, became the last French winner of Wimbledon, a distinction that stands to this day. That tennis player was also the last to wear long pants on the court. My grandfather was convinced that he had respected this sartorial tradition to the end in the manner of the children of Chợ Lớn, who not only adhered to millenary customs and mores but spoke Vietnamese with a Chinese accent, even if they had never set foot in China.

My father never liked Chợ Lớn. He preferred downtown Saigon with its French cafés and American bars. Above all, he liked to drink beer on the Hôtel

Continental terrace, where the foreign journalists spent their days analyzing troop movements and the latest popular songs. As often as he could, he reserved the table where Graham Greene, a war correspondent at the beginning of the 1950s, liked to station himself to keep an eye on the city and to draw inspiration from neighbouring tables for the characters in his novel *The Quiet American.*

AT THE HEIGHT OF THE LÊ VĂN AN EMPIRE,
my grandfather collected dwellings situated on the
Hai Bà Trưng Street of different towns through
which he passed. He wanted to remind my aunts that
they should be independent of mind and above all
combative, following the example of the two Trưng
sisters, who had driven back the Chinese army and
governed sixty-five towns and villages for three years,
before committing suicide when they lost power. In
honour of those two heroines who remained
unrivalled for two thousand years, my grandfather
offered the use of those houses to nieces, cousins,
friends, and scholarship holders during their studies.
Over the years, the beneficiaries transformed those
temporary lodgings into permanent residences when
they started their families.

My father took possession of the house on Hai Bà
Trưng Street in Saigon, where he hosted his mistresses
and friends. They got together for games of Ping-
Pong or poker with their paramour of the day, or for
"forbidden games," as he liked to call them, referring
to the soundtrack of the famous French film and its
melody that was learned by all the Vietnamese youths
who tried to coax songs from their guitars. Once married, he continued to use this space for the same pur-
poses, as did many of the men in his circle. Out of
discretion and in the interests of her own survival, my
mother never set foot there. She just reminded the
servant to always have ready a dish of fresh fruit, to

prepare dried shrimp mixed with marinated wild garlic cloves to accompany the rice wine, and to bring along baguettes and pâté to be consumed along with the wine.

This servant was and still is my father's closest friend. They were born three months apart. His mother had been hired as my father's wet nurse by my maternal grandmother, who didn't know that the young woman had left her village to continue her pregnancy to term. The two boys became brothers. They played marbles together, engaged in cricket battles and sword fights. They raised fighting fish, one per jar, keeping each one hidden from the other with pieces of cardboard to save their energies for battle. Sometimes they allowed themselves to lift the cardboard and admire the deployment of their fins. The blue one fanned its tail into a half moon; the white one swept the water with its skirts as if its long wedding dress were as light as air; the orange one was less spectacular, but very precious because it never gave up; as much as the orange attacked, so the yellow was master of the art of evading its adversary and waiting patiently for the opportune moment to strike. The two boys spent hours discussing the personalities of their fish, and feeding them mosquito larvae. Their passion for the fish from the stagnant water of the rice paddies never waned. Their collection grew as soon as they were able to raise females as well, and knew how to pair them with a male during their fertile periods.

They watched closely as the males made their nests of bubbles in preparation for the births and chased off the females as soon as they'd laid their eggs. The boys then transferred them to another jar to prevent the females from devouring their children. They raised their fish together, like a family that belonged exclusively to them. They had their favourites, but were deeply saddened when any one of them died.

MY FATHER AND HIS SERVANT were brothers who
had different family names and different parents, and
who went to different schools. One attended the
neighbourhood school with its beaten earth floor
while the other carried his notebooks in a bag made
of elephant hide. Everyone knew my father's school,
which was named for Pétrus Ky, an intellectual who
had taught and popularized the Vietnamese language
written with the Roman alphabet instead of Chinese
characters. Even though Vietnamese is now written by
sound, most of the words still carry the trace of the
original images from ideograms.

My first name, Bảo Vi, showed my parents' deter-
mination to "protect the smallest one." In a literal
translation, I am "Tiny precious microscopic." As is
often the case in Vietnam, I did not match the image
of my own name. Girls called "Blanche" (Bạch) or
"Snow" (Tuyết) will have very dark skin, and boys
called "Powerful" (Hùng) or "Strong" (Mạnh) will be
afraid of challenges. As for me, I kept on growing, far
surpassing the average and at the same time projecting
myself outside the norm. Teachers put me in the back
row so they would have a better overall view of the
classroom. In that way they could detect the slightest
out-of-place movement and the guilty student would
end up instantly at the board, facing his sixty classmates, hand open, waiting for the blow of the wooden
ruler on his knuckles or palm. Afterwards, it was
extremely difficult for the pupil to hold a pen, dip it

into the ink bottle, and write without trembling. In spite of his efforts and the pink blotter held in the left hand to follow the movements of the pen and soak up excess ink, he was rarely able to follow the two-millimetre horizontal lines in the ruled Séyès notebooks without going over the edge or staining the paper. Besides having a swollen hand, he would lose points for sloppy work. I was definitely a model student compared with the scatterbrains relegated to the back of the classroom. Or at least the most delicate, because I tried as best I could to be a "Vi," a microscopic girl, invisible.

If my father had been as invisible as me at the end of the war, he would not have been arrested and sent to a re-education camp in the region of Thủ Đức, where he shared with the ten comrades in his hut his daily ration of ten peanuts. Because my father had been born with the destiny of princes, he was freed after two months. His servant brother had been able to save him by demonstrating to the authorities that my father had supported him financially in his espionage work for the Communist resistance. He argued that my father had indirectly helped the North to win the war against the South, which had exonerated him from the status of bourgeois capitalist. Without the intervention of that enemy brother, he'd have stayed behind digging canals, clearing minefields, digging up the ground with the other prisoners who had lost all hope of learning when they would be set free. The only thought they allowed themselves was to hope that a grasshopper or a rat would happen by and become their evening meal, because any other reflection could be interpreted as a betrayal of Communist thought. The surgeon in the next hut, who had been drying a few tiny rice cakes in the sun, was accused of preparing for his escape instead of concentrating on his re-education. An accountant had been similarly sanctioned when he confided to the other prisoners that he could hear the sound of motorcycles driving along the north side of the prison. If my father had seen other men being summoned by the guards, never to come back to the camp, he might perhaps have chosen to flee Vietnam. Perhaps he would not have abandoned us to our race towards the unknown without him. Like my mother, he would perhaps have given priority to saving his sons from military service. Unfortunately, once again he withdrew into the cocoon of his bachelor apartment, isolated from the uncertainties of life.

WE LEFT VIETNAM with a close friend of my mother, Hà, and her parents.

Hà is much younger than my mother. At the beginning of the 1970s in Saigon, she was the perfect modern woman in the American style, with her very short dresses that showed off the slanted, heart-shaped birthmark high up on her left thigh. I remember her irresistible platform shoes in the hallway of our house, which struck me as decadent, or at least gave me a new perspective on the world when I slipped them on. Her false eyelashes thick with mascara transformed her eyes into two spiky-haired rambutans. She was our Twiggy, with her apple-green and turquoise eye-shadow, two colours that clashed with her coppery skin. She was unlike most of the young girls, who avoided the sun in order to set themselves apart from the peasants in the rice fields, who had to roll their pants up to their knees and endure the violent bright light. Hà bared her skin at the swimming pool of the very exclusive Cercle Sportif, where she gave me swimming lessons. She preferred American freedom to the elegance of French culture, which gave her the courage to participate in the first Miss Vietnam competition, even though she was an English teacher.

My mother did not approve of her choices, which went contrary to her status as a well-educated young woman from a good family. But she supported her by buying her the long dress and bathing suit that Hà would wear on stage. She had her practise walking in a straight line along the tiled floor, balancing a dictionary on her head, as she'd seen women do in films. My mother treated her as if she were her big sister, and shielded her from gossip. She allowed Hà to take me with her to the chic boutiques on rue Catinat, and to drink a lime soda with her foreign friends. Hà marched along this street with its grand hotels like a proud conqueror. The city belonged to her. I wondered whether my mother envied her this ease that came from the compliments raining down on her from her teachers and her American colleagues. The latter celebrated her beauty with gifts of chocolate bars, hair curlers, and Louis Armstrong records, whereas the Vietnamese looked on her dark complexion as "savage." More than once, my grandparents asked my mother to halt my swimming lessons with Hà. I suspect that my mother disobeyed them and kept Hà close to us because she hoped I'd learn to be beautiful. Unfortunately, that time with Hà in Vietnam was too short—or my apprenticeship, too slow.

IN 1954, THE SEVENTEENTH PARALLEL cut
Vietnam in two. In 1975, April 30 drew a line divid-
ing before from after, between the end of a war and
what followed, between power and fear. Before, we
heard Hà's laughter as soon as she turned off her
scooter's motor. She laughed while playing hopscotch
with the children in the alley, she teased the gardener
for the irresistible transparency of his worn shirt, she
fearlessly answered to the yapping of our guard dogs.
After, Hà became the wife of a general from Vinh, a
northern town razed by bombings but filled with wan-
dering spirits, including those of his parents, whom
he'd not been able to visit again before they became
buried beneath the ruins. Without that general, all of
Hà's family would have been sent to the uninhabitable
swampy lands called "new economic zones."

Becoming the wife of a general allowed Hà to continue teaching English, and not have to line up to buy
the monthly ration of sugar, rice, and meat. No one
dared to speak badly of those who had made the
same choice as Hà. But the stares of others wounded
her as much as the general's slaps, to which she was
resigned. She couldn't spare her parents the noises
betraying her submission, since they were just on the
other side of a newly installed curtain. Rather than
leap up in a rage, her parents kept silent. They played
dead. They feared that Hà might suffer the same fate
as their neighbour, who had put a bullet into her
head after having succeeded in freeing her husband

from a re-education camp in exchange for a liaison with a high-ranking officer from the North. This new partner had consented to the liberation and also to her husband's and children's flight by boat. After their departure, she pulled the trigger to achieve her own liberation.

My mother treated this new Hà, in her dark clothes and no longer wearing makeup, with the same consideration as before. She awaited her with cotton batten and the bottle of lotion she used to treat her every wound. According to family lore, this long infusion of rice wine and medicinal herbs had healed a cousin's neck that had been torn open by shrapnel from a bomb, prevented a neighbour's burns from becoming infected after she had been doused with acid by a jealous husband, and could make bruises vanish even before your tears had dried.

As much as Hà had proudly displayed her painted eyelids before her marriage to the general, so, from the start of her new relationship, she hid her black eyes under the wide brim of a hat. I had the impression that she was becoming smaller and smaller, not only because of her flat plastic slippers that scraped the ground, but also because of the absence of her boisterous laughter. She climbed the steps like a shadow, to blend in properly with the silence that prevailed all across the country. Keyholes gave access to no secret conversations. The drifting winds bore no words or music. Nothing was airborne but the government messages blaring from loudspeakers, reminding us that it was the day of the great cleanup, when all the neighbourhood residents had to bring out their brooms at the same time to clean the streets; or announcing a court case to be judged by three neighbours, bringing accusations against a former lawyer who had dared to cite the Napoleonic Code during a discussion; or denouncing families who had celebrated a marriage too joyfully or who had mourned too sorrowfully the loss of a dear one . . . I didn't know that my mother took advantage of these public proclamations to whisper into Hà's ear the address of a smuggler who would organize our departure from Vietnam.

HÀ CROSSED THE GULF of Siam at the same time we did. She had managed to persuade the hairdresser to introduce her to her cousin, who worked for someone who knew someone who could recommend an organizer. No name and no promise had been given. In exchange for the gold taels demanded for her passage and that of her parents, she had been told to go to the hair salon as often as possible in order to learn the departure dates. This was how she became my mother's messenger.

We took the same bus at dawn on a morning that was supposed to seem like all others, my father still in bed and my mother in motion, noiselessly performing task after task. She put on my street clothes over two pairs of pants. I obeyed all of her instructions. I already knew that I was to ask no questions so as not to disturb her steady gaze, which served as a barrier to her tears. I can still see her rubbing my brothers' nails with charcoal, unlike all the other days when a nurse filed them while another sang to distract them. As for my mother, she was wearing the clothes of our herb seller.

During the trip from Saigon to the water, I kept my face flattened against her blouse, still impregnated with the scent of lemon balm, which refused to give way to that of coriander. This mixture of perfumes in the bus put me to sleep, sparing me the gouts of blood from the fish that the passenger standing near us was carrying in a bag, which sometimes dripped onto me when the vehicle veered to the left. Sleep prevented me from being afraid of the policeman who asked Hà and my brother Long, sitting two rows behind us, for their identification papers. Before dropping off, I saw Hà's father slip some money into the hands of the one who was reproaching my brother Loc for wearing his hair long, the way capitalists did, a rebellious act that warranted a prison sentence.

WE COVERED three hundred kilometres in ten hours.
Towards the end of the trip, I didn't hear the chickens
anymore, clucking away in unison along with the noisy
cạp cạp cạp of the ducks on the roof, shut into their
woven rattan cage. The first time I ever ate Peking
duck, our waiter meticulously sliced off pieces of skin
that we sampled in rolls minus the meat, and I couldn't
help thinking about those ducks. I wondered if their
skin also came off their flesh beneath the fiery heat of
the roof, like the Peking duck's, like mine, so puffy
after the long trip. My feet had swollen in the dense
and stagnant heat of the bus, overflowing the shoes'
thongs, stretching my skin to the point of transparency.

When I was small and still extremely sensitive to
changes in temperature, my father, when there was a
power failure, settled me into our air-conditioned car
to put me to sleep. He would lay me down beside him,
then drive through the city. His hand caressed my
damp hair, and he said: "My daughter is fermenting
like yogurt." As well, he compared my hands to balls
of dough, the little brioches that my mother and I prepared together every Sunday. According to my father,
even Parisian bakers could not compete with my
mother. What was more, even if he ate in the best restaurants in town, he insisted that no chef knew how to
lift stuffed zucchini blossoms from the frying pan the
way she did, just in time to preserve the texture of the
petals. Only my mother had mastered their preparation and knew how to extract their sugar beneath the

crisp, light crust of rice flour. Like other Vietnamese families, we put all the dishes out in the middle of the table at the same time, with one exception. My mother served my father separately, in order to save the best for him: the soft-shelled crab overflowing with eggs, the perfectly shaped sticks of fried potatoes, the most tender chicory leaves. It went without saying that the fifty seeds of the sugar apple were removed, and its sweet white flesh held out to him like an offering.

MY FATHER INTRODUCED US to delicacies brought
back from elsewhere, such as aniseed from Flavigny or
foie gras, or the cantaloupes that were served in certain French restaurants in Saigon. He insisted on celebrating Christmas with yule logs and welcoming
friends more often with chocolate éclairs than with
black sesame or banana candies. For my third birthday, the cook was ordered to prepare a three-tiered
cake with buttercream. Usually I was more attracted
to rice and taro puddings or to ice cream served in
brioche. That day, impelled by some mysterious desire,
I bit into the first tier as soon as the cake had been
placed on its stand. No one could believe that I was
capable of an act so decadent and spontaneous. My
father blamed the dog, which was tied up ten metres
from the kitchen.

I rediscovered this same outlandish and uncontrol-
lable craving the first time I bit into a Belgian waffle. I
recognized the texture of the dough and the taste of
the granular sugar described by my father, who had
been seduced by the aroma of melted butter at a
waffle stand in the Brussels train station. I heard his
voice when I strolled past the Bruges boutiques, where
he had purchased a lace shawl for my mother. At the
time, my father's travelling companion preferred to
offer some fabric to his wife, who immediately turned
it into an *áo dài*. The next day she saw a young
weather reporter on television wearing the identical
outfit. And yet this cloth was impossible to find in

Vietnam. She tried to include my mother in her jealous rage, imagining a number of different scenarios for taking a wrathful revenge, from a confrontation to a denunciation in the newspaper. While this woman was certainly correct in believing that my mother was the victim of similar conjugal transgressions, my mother remained impassive during her fit of anger. She only advised her not to humiliate herself by humiliating her husband's mistress. Then she draped her lace shawl, as fragile as a breath of air, over her *áo dài* of silk, to attend a reception in honour of her father-in-law, Judge Lê Văn An. Her ears were adorned with the pair of pearls offered by her mother-in-law on the occasion of the birth of my twin brothers. Were she to encounter another woman wearing the same shawl, she would greet her with the self-assurance that she was the mother of the four children bearing the name of my father.

One day, while I was napping in a hammock, my mother received the visit of a young woman with a child my age called Trí. Through the netting, I watched him shooting marbles. Bits of their conversation reached my ears, even though they were whispering. Before falling back to sleep, I saw my mother place in the young woman's palm her gold necklace and bracelet, and I heard her tell the young woman to return to Cà Mau and to never again try to disturb my father.

CÀ MAU, known for the blackness of its swampy waters and its dense, dark forest, is located at the extreme southerly point of Vietnam. Surrounded by three seas, it is perfectly placed for flights by boat. We hid there with my half-brother, Trí, waiting for a sign from our smuggler. His mother, she who wore my mother's chain around her neck, fed us for the two days preceding our departure. My mother offered to take Trí with us. Amid the chaos of fear, the silence and the darkness, Trí got on a different boat than ours with Hà, who had lost her parents in the crowd. We left Vietnam in three different boats. Ours docked in Malaysia without having encountered any storms or pirates. Hà and Trí didn't have the same luck. Their boat was intercepted by pirates four times. During the last attack, Trí received an accidental machete blow from a man in an agitated state. My mother lied to his mother, saying that he was reported missing at sea along with Hà's parents. My father never found out that he had lost a son.

MY FIRST NAME did not prepare me for facing storms on the high seas, and even less for sharing a straw hut in a Malaysian refugee camp with an elderly woman who cried day and night for a month without telling us the identity of the fourteen young children who accompanied her. We had to wait for the farewell meal on the eve of our departure for Canada before she suddenly related to us the details of her crossing. She had seen her son's throat being cut before her eyes because he'd dared to throw himself on a pirate who was raping his pregnant wife. This mother had fainted at the moment when her son and daughter-in-law were thrown into the sea. She didn't know what happened next. She only remembered waking up beneath bodies, to the sound of tears being shed by the fourteen surviving children.

When the words began to pass between the pallid lips of this woman who was more like a ghost, my mother chased me from the hut in an attempt to safeguard the innocence of my eight years. It was a futile gesture, since the walls were made from jute bags and the ceilings from canvas. In any case, similar stories were being told around the well, in the dust, during our sleep, everywhere in the camp. I knew that we had to avoid the two men suspected of cannibalism during their voyage, and not to disturb the statue-woman who waited religiously from dawn to dusk for her baby to wash up on the beach.

My mother became the de facto leader of the

women with no husbands, because she demanded that my brothers help other mothers by bringing them containers of water.

When we had arrived in the camp, the French and Australian delegations had just left. No one could tell us when they might return, or when delegations from other countries might be passing through. It went without saying that no refugee planned to live long-term in the camp. But our daily tasks rooted us, despite everything, in this hot and hostile land. New rituals fell into place: young boys got together at dusk around a palm tree whose trunk followed the horizontal incline of the ground, to play with marbles offered by one of the Malaysian supervisors; new lovers escaped behind the big rocks on the hill; artists sculpted pieces of the wreckage from boats. Quite soon, dragging one's empty pail for three hours to reach the well became as banal as the pains from chronic dysentery. The discomfort of physical and mental proximity diminished, to the rhythm of spontaneous laughter and miraculous reunions. In this isolated world, friendships were born of the simplest bond. Two classmates became two sisters, two natives of the same town helped each other out as if they were cousins, two orphans formed a family.

THE CANADIAN DELEGATION was the first to receive us. My mother had organized a class in the camp. She taught mathematics in French to children, and the French language to adults. She had the good fortune to be taken on as an interpreter by the francophone delegations during the selection sessions. She didn't know that the Canadian delegation offered interpreters the opportunity to immigrate. Because we were part of the first large wave of Vietnamese immigrants allowed into Canada, we had heard no rumours about the country, which we assumed was wintry for all twelve months of the year. My mother assured us that our Đà Lạt roots would help us adapt to the cold. To me, she said that Santa Claus lived at the North Pole, very near to Canada.

WE ARRIVED in the city of Quebec during a heat wave that seemed to have undressed the entire population. The men sitting on the balconies of our new domicile were all stripped to the waist with their bellies well in view, like the Budai, those laughing Buddhas who promised financial success to merchants and to others joy, if they rubbed their roundness. Many Vietnamese men dreamed of possessing this symbol of wealth, but few succeeded. My brother Long could not help expressing his happiness when our bus stopped in front of a row of buildings where abundance was on show many times over. "We've landed in paradise!"

LONG GOT BUSY finding us clothes more suited to the season, because my mother had bought only warm clothing from the itinerant Malaysian peddler, anticipating a cold Canada. She had been happy and proud to have found for me, in the wheelbarrow-boutique, a pair of red fake-leather boots, whose gloss made you overlook the torn lining inside. The right heel, worn down unevenly, gave me the walk of the little girl who must have got rid of the boots after wearing them for quite a while, since the zippers had been mended several times. She became my imaginary friend, who urged me to put one foot in front of the other in a totally new world that frightened me, with its space and its far horizons.

Like the chickens that boat-dwelling families raised in the hollow middle of thick lengths of bamboo, I preferred to stay motionless in our apartment, much too vast compared with our small plot of earth in the refugee camp. My body had adapted itself to the shape of my brothers and my mother. I'd slept surrounded by their arms, their ribs, and the unevenness of the ground. How to find oneself alone one day atop the softness of a mattress without being cocooned in the sweat of my family, without being lulled by their breath? How to suddenly lose the permanent presence of my mother? How to find one's way before an endless horizon, with no barbed wire, no overseers?

Given the absence of addresses in the refugee camp, we had resorted to visual aids: the woman who lends out needles has an enamel water pail with a handle; the German interpreter sleeps under a blue clothesline mended with rags; the hairdresser has a mirror nailed to a skinny tree trunk. To locate the dressmaker, you have to go past the rock where the monk meditates at dawn, turn left at the well, circle the latrines, and ask neighbours and passersby where she may be found. And so, with my eyes still unaccustomed to the vastness, how could I find my way in the midst of the wide, long boulevard whose trees all seemed perfectly identical?

AS THE ELDEST, my brother Long bore the burden
of acting as head of the family. He took the place of
both my father and my mother. He took care of us
while my mother washed dishes at the corner restaurant until midnight. He taught us our address, our
telephone number, and showed us how to greet people
in French. He introduced himself to the neighbours
and was friendly with them. He smiled at all the
people he met, without exception: the lady on the
ground floor behind her walker; the grasshopper-
children on the third floor; the tattooed man; the
young girl in her miniskirt and high heels. He opened
doors and helped people carry their grocery bags. He
swept up the cigarette butts, advertising circulars, and
candy wrappers on the stairs. He played ball with the
children. Within a few weeks, the whole neighbourhood knew his name. His years of apprenticeship in
French in Saigon schools enabled him to grasp very
quickly how the public transit system worked.

He made his way through the city by bus, and
asked the drivers, with confidence and pride, "May I
have a *transport*, please?" And he was given a coupon
to present to the next driver, which would let him
continue on his way to the centre of town.

My hero-brother persuaded the owner of a Japanese
restaurant to hire him. He started as a busboy, and
was soon promoted to the job of juggling utensils
behind the hot plate. He transported the diners all the
way to Kobe, a place where he'd never set foot. His

acrobatic manipulation of the ingredients lent him a Japanese identity. While his clients were realizing their dreams of exoticism, my brother Long was making his way towards the realization of dreams of his own.

BEFORE ARRIVING in Canada, I knew only one
initialism: UNHCR. The High Commissioner collab-
orated with the Malaysian Red Cross to deliver water
and food to more than 250,000 Vietnamese refugees
found in camps scattered all across Malaysia, and
more particularly on the island of Pulau Bidong,
where nearly 60,000 people lived. Many people were
deployed throughout the territory to offer us shelter
from the sun, the rain, and also from the coconuts,
which were abundant on the island. Despite these
precautions, a woman had been struck on the head
by a coconut and lapsed into a coma. She had been
washing her coconut-shell bowls and ladles when the
accident happened. A representative of the Canadian
delegation had tried to transport her to the hospital,
but on account of a storm, the dinghy had not been
able to reach the boat that would have taken them to
dry land. This woman had survived the crossing of
the Gulf of Siam, deprived of water and food for several weeks. She had been spared by pirates when they
found her hiding in an oil drum. Unfortunately, she
lost her battle with destiny during the night. She died
with no family and no country.

Unlike the fate that befell this woman, life guided
us all the way to Canada. When we heard the news,
I remember Long lifting me up to do a somersault in
the air. As soon as we arrived on 3rd Avenue in the
Limoilou neighbourhood, he wanted to get us on the
right track by enrolling us in school as quickly as

possible. He met with the teachers, oversaw our home-work, and dreamed of a future for all of us. While Long had the charisma of my father and the daring of our mother, his twin, Lộc, and our brother Linh pre-ferred to stay in the background. In the beginning, Long wanted them to study engineering, like all the Vietnamese students who had arrived in the 1960s. But Lộc chose to follow in the footsteps of a Quebec philanthropist who inspired him to become an oncolo-gist. As for Linh, he seemed to have been born to spend his days and nights as a computer programmer. Long studied business, and capitalized on his experi-ence to become the manager of the Kobe restaurant. As soon as he got his degree, his employer put him in charge of the second and third Kobe franchises in town. Later, he would invest in the creation of an Asian restaurant chain in shopping malls.

At university, he became active in community life. It was rare to have no guests around our table, as our apartment became the meeting place for Vietnamese students editing a newspaper or setting up a soccer, badminton, or Ping-Pong team with a view to partici-pating in the Vietnamese North American Olympics.

Aside from the boots in the entrance hall and the winter coats piled on the beds, we might have thought we were back in Saigon. The typical aroma of Vietnamese kitchens scented the air, thanks to my mother. She immersed us in the odour of chopped and roasted citronella wed to crisp fish skin, or in that of young sprigs of bamboo sautéed then dipped in lime-flavoured fish sauce. The complicated dishes she served us took a long time to prepare; she wanted to feed us well, but she could not have done it without the help of Hoa, Long's beloved.

HOA SHADOWED my brother Long from their very first philosophy class in college. She always brought along a second serving for him when he was in a meeting during lunch hour. Long had inherited from our father a beauty that attracted as many men as women. His friends wanted nothing more than to follow him around because he fulfilled their dreams. A boy who was studying science while suppressing his dream of becoming a singer was invited to organize an evening of Vietnamese songs in the space where theatre classes were given. The future doctor could then experience the joy of being onstage along with his friends who would have liked to be guitarists or dancers. A girl who explored the world through drawing was invited to contribute to the newspaper since her talent had no outlet in her chemistry and physics courses. Those young people who came first in their classes were sometimes secret poets whom Long allowed to sign their texts with a pseudonym so their parents would be none the wiser.

Unlike those students, Hoa concentrated on her courses in nursing without harbouring any particular dream or talent. On the other hand, she was extremely adept and discreet in staying close to Long without getting in his way. Her greatest asset was responding to the needs and expectations of our mother. Long had always acceded to her demands even when they were unreasonable, for he knew the magnitude of what she had lost.

BÁT TRÀNG

~

bát = bowl;
tràng = territory,
land, place

My mother strictly supervised the size of Hoa's crushed ice crystals before they were added to the glasses of coffee prepared in the Vietnamese way, that is, drop by drop. In Vietnam, the crushed ice was sold in narrow blocks more than a metre long. Here, Hoa had to create these blocks using condensed milk cans instead of ice trays. According to my mother, the shape of the ice influenced the taste of the coffee, just like the thickness of the shreds of roast pork when she was preparing the *bì*. She removed from Hoa's cutting board the pieces that were more than a millimetre wide to cut them further, and took the knife out of Hoa's hands if she accidentally pierced a chicken's skin while deboning it. Every time the grocery stores had whole chickens on sale, the house would overflow with activity. Our mother would buy at least five, and spend a good part of the night deboning them completely before stuffing them through the smallest possible opening, so they would not collapse.

From time to time Long organized picnics, and often he chose to serve this dish to his friends, who only had to cut a slice to have an entire meal on their plate. They did not suspect that each mouthful involved hours of work, humility, and obedience on the part of Hoa. She had to follow my mother's strict orders concerning the two stages of cooking the rice for the stuffing, the size of the Vietnamese sausage cubes once they were cooked, the proper quantity of shiitake mushrooms, whose scent must enhance without being invasive . . . Hoa endured in silence all my mother's demands, even when I was alone with her, peeling the skins off peanuts, one by one. Patiently, she showed me how to roll an empty bottle over the nuts in order to crush them without reducing them to powder.

I wondered whether her discretion derived from the long tradition in Bát Tràng, her hometown, of working clay to produce fragile porcelain, or from her acceptance of being born weak. Hoa knew in advance that university would be difficult for her, if not impossible. Her only hope was that Long would give her a chance to express her love. As with her profession as a nurse, she expected nothing in return, neither from her patients nor from Long, especially not a formal proposal of marriage, made on her birthday.

HOA'S RETIRING PERSONALITY could also be attributed to her stay in a crowded camp in Hong Kong, where simply taking a breath impinged on another's territory. Like all the refugees, she'd learned very quickly how to disappear into a bubble to be alone. The first time I heard in Quebec the expression "You're in my bubble," I thought the person addressing me was making a declaration of friendship by permitting me to share his thoughts, his inner space, when what he in fact wanted was for me to back off, back away. Unlike in Western culture, which encourages expressions of feelings and opinions, the Vietnamese keep them jealously to themselves, and speak of them with great reluctance, because this inner space is the only one inaccessible to others. All the rest, from academic grades to salaries to sleep, is in the public domain, as are love affairs.

I WONDER IF THE openness regarding personal
details derives from the tropical temperatures that dis-
courage the shutting of doors, windows, and walls;
the lack of space between the two or three generations
living under the same roof; the dependence on family
ties; or whether it's the weight of family history, which
must be borne out of gratitude, and sometimes as a
burden. The child's success belongs to his parents and
ancestors. Every family member is responsible for all
the others, out of solidarity. The stronger support the
weaker. Otherwise, any personal success would be
marred by an inadequate sense of duty and honouring
of the clan. In the same way, each individual feels and
displays guilt as a result of others' mistakes. I remember a man with his son and daughter who went on
their knees before my mother because of a theft his
wife had committed. He'd brought back the two gold
chains with bells attached that my mother had put
around my ankles so she could hear me running in the
house. I'd held out my feet to my mother, but she'd
knelt down to attach the jewels to the ankles of the two
children still on their knees. I never saw that nurse-
maid again, who was guilty not only of theft but, above
all, of the shame with which she had burdened her
children. My mother often told us that we were lucky
to have parents who would never commit fraud or
other unseemly acts. But sometimes, even honest parents cannot resist the pressures exerted by the history
of a people, passed on from one generation to another.

A friend of my mother's, a former teacher, told us one winter's night that in one of her classes in Nha Trang, a young student whose father had fought with the South and an equally young student whose father had sided with the North fell deeply in love before learning about the family history on either side, because they had grown up after the reconciliation of North and South. When the two mothers heard the news, they asked to meet the teacher so that she might help them prohibit a union between enemies. The mothers also appealed to the friends of their children, hoping they might urge them to separate. One day, as the caretaker was sweeping the courtyard with the constant and repetitive sound of reeds scraping the cement, the boy's mother burst into the classroom and threw herself in front of the blackboard, crying out, over and over: "He is dead!" The students' tears joined her cries, the noise escaping through the windows to cross the yard and reach the other rooms.

Everyone cried, except for the young girl who was in love. Her eyes stayed dry, and her body upright. She left school at the end of the day along with her classmates, walking steadily, her breathing regular, her body language and gestures normal. She calmly held out the coupon to the attendant in order to retrieve her bicycle, wheeling it beside her to the exit before placing her conical hat on her head, the strap under her chin. She pulled on the rear panel of her *áo dài*, holding it in her right hand as she lowered herself onto the old leather seat with the gracefulness of youth, and pedalled away. Her face betrayed no emotion, nor did the steady rhythm of her legs. From far off, she resembled all the other students, whom romantics compared to white butterflies. The adolescents knew that together they were an embellishment to the streets as they left their classes with their uniforms in movement. The student, whose heart was not broken but stopped, deviated in no way from this virginal beauty. She arrived home and greeted her mother, who awaited her with a snack of gac fruit sticky rice—a square cake on which the word "happiness" is carved in Chinese, and which newlyweds offer to guests during the marriage ceremony at the altar of their ancestors.

The orange hue of the perfumed rice, tinted by the flesh of the gac, could get lost in the bright-red abundance of the tablecloths, the decorations, and the bride's dress. But the guests always found them, since the gac only ripened once a year. Out-of-season marriages had to bypass this fruit of paradise, as some called it. That is why her mother had been very happy to receive, as a guest at a wedding, this rich, orange-hued cake. She presented it as an offering to her daughter, who thanked her politely, tracing the word "happiness" with her finger for fifteen minutes without eating it. The teacher had followed her student to the house. Since many Vietnamese houses were completely open, with the ground floor often transformed into a commercial space during the day, she felt at the same time as her student's mother that an emptiness had arrived that sucked all the air out of the room.

Suddenly, the motorcycle horns, the noise of the two rollers compressing the stalks of sugar cane at the neighbour's, the chatter of the customers awaiting their glass of juice— all went silent. It was only when the young girl's body landed on the pavement that her mother and the teacher cried out. They tried to revive her by rubbing her temples and feet with tiger balm, but were unable to bring her back to consciousness. The teacher offered to stay with her student that night. The mother reminded her that it was useful to watch over the living, but that nothing could be done for the dead. Even if the young student had never been allowed to read *Romeo and Juliet*, or see the film *Love Story*, or hear of *Tristan and Isolde*, even though her literary knowledge was restricted to the biography of Ho Chi Minh and some war heroes, even if the decorations pinned to her father's uniform guaranteed her a privileged future, she had chosen to join her love. She had freed herself from the burdensome history that was the legacy of a war she had not known, by walking towards the beauty of Nha Trang's sublime sea.

ALL THROUGH MY EARLY CHILDHOOD, we went to the sea almost every month for "a change of wind," as my father said. The salt water miraculously healed the cracked skin on my grandmother's heels, and cleared up my own frequently congested nose. The salt air helped my brothers grow, and amplified our laughter around the dried cuttlefish sold on the beach by itinerant merchants. Two cuttlefish, perfectly flat and grilled over a few red coals, fed the whole family for the whole afternoon, since they were eaten strand by strand. The taste of these elastic filaments lasted longer than a stick of Juicy Fruit in my mouth. Those joyous and light-hearted moments in the sand did not prevent me from fearing the sea, as much for its vastness as for its depth and its beauty. My father strung the most beautiful floats around my waist, and pushed me towards the moving waters. I thought I would die every time a wave took me away from my father's breath on my neck. He turned the duck's head of my float towards the horizon, thinking that the smooth surface would calm me. He also pivoted me in the other direction so that I could see our beach umbrella and my mother hidden behind a big hat and her sunglasses, with a towel on her head. The two points of view paralyzed me. That unhealthy fear would remain with me, until the day we learned that the ocean had not swallowed up Hà's boat.

After several weeks at sea with a failed engine, and with the refugees running low on food, her boat was rescued by a Danish freighter and Hà went directly to Copenhagen without passing through the camps and without meeting the other passengers again, for fear of seeing in their eyes the reflection of her own body, which had been subjected to multiple rapes. Thanks to her knowledge of English, she was able to integrate easily, working in hotels, where she learned about massage therapy. After taking some courses, she reinvented herself as a massage therapist. The clients said that she repaired their bodies. Very quickly, her calendar filled up a month in advance. She lengthened her working hours in order to accommodate everybody. But one day she refused to treat a man after he had filled out his health form. His name was Louis. There was nothing special about him, but something in his look had unsettled her. She said that she'd had to clench her fists in order to hide her fingers, which were shaking like the leaves of a poplar tree.

In Denmark, she was able to concentrate on the well-being of others. She was able to detect disappointment in a deltoid, shame in a latissimus dorsal, resignation in a gluteus medius . . . She sought out all the sorrows in the muscle fibres in order to alleviate them and, when possible, eliminate them by repeating her mother's movements, seizing the pain of her little girl's wounds in her hand and tossing it in the air to make it disappear. Her fingers had the gift not only of hypnotizing her clients but also of leaving the weight of their impressions on the skin long after the end of the session. She always refused to be massaged by her colleagues, however. She feared that the pressure of a hand on her skin would shatter her fissured body. She wouldn't know how to reassemble the pieces, or to put some order into the thousand fragments that would have been spread out before her, like a town after a hurricane has passed through. Her clients found her serene, gentle, even wise, while Louis had immediately sensed her extreme fragility, and the chaos dormant within her, awaiting the first sign of weakness to undo everything. Louis waited until a stormy night, until the last day of the year, to approach her in a bus shelter, and offer her some tea. After a long day putting bodies into balance, assuming her clients' wounds, Hà felt her legs give way. Louis caught her and loved her.

HÀ FOLLOWED Louis to Ottawa, where he returned
at the end of his mandate in Copenhagen. She found
my mother by looking for the names of her relatives
in all the telephone directories. Louis brought her to
our door. Hà and my mother talked through that
first night. I heard them weep, and sometimes go
silent. During the long conversation, the word "luck"
returned again and again, as they described the
experiences and the ordeals they had lived through.
Once she found love with Louis, Hà began offering
massage therapy to damaged women, women in dis-
tress and without resources in shelters. She also helped
them to look at themselves in the mirror, to listen to a
Bee Gees song with her, or to choose an article of
clothing in the collective wardrobe, to be worn for job
interviews. It was thanks to the friendship of those
women that she dared to start counting the number
of slaps received, the number of pirates encountered,
the number of steps that had separated her from her
parents on that night of escape.

I DISCOVERED MANHATTAN when I was thirteen.
Hà took me there with Louis for a weekend. She'd
suggested to my mother that I come to stay with her
during the holidays. My mother gave her permission to
look after me as if I were her daughter. Hà began by
unbuttoning the collar and sleeves of my blouses. In restaurants, she demanded that I choose between the ham-
burger and the pizza. Between vanilla and chocolate,
between apple juice and a milkshake. Then came the
choice of colours for the walls of the guest bedroom so
it would become mine as of the second year of Ottawa
visits. Like my brother Long, Louis and Hà entertained
often and had many friends. Louis made it his mission
to bring me out of the kitchen and introduce me to the
guests. When they arrived, he supported me by placing
his hand in the middle of my back, while at the end of
the meal he placed it on my shoulder to stop me from
getting up and collecting the plates. During the evening, he always suspended the conversation at an opportune moment, inserting a question that forced me to
give an answer, to be wholly present. It was with them
that I learned of the existence of Burundi, Chile,
Morocco, Sri Lanka, Guadeloupe, and also NATO, the
OECD, and the International Court of Justice. Louis had
friends from many different backgrounds, often
nomads because of their diplomatic jobs. Or, on the
contrary, they had chosen to be diplomats in order to
live everywhere in the world without ever becoming
citizens, without ever belonging to a single place.

My brother Long often reproached my mother for having entrusted me to Hà and Louis, since the stable and easy path he'd imagined for me in pharmacology or medicine had been replaced by a career that would prove unpredictable and chaotic.

WHILE LOUIS was posted to Shanghai, Hà offered me an airplane ticket so I could join them during the summer holidays. I spent my winter and spring evenings studying Chinese from a book I found at the local library. It contained an analysis of a thousand characters classified according to the number of strokes in each one. To my great surprise, the character for the number one, a single horizontal stroke, was considered the most important, because it illustrated the primordial unity, the fusion between sky and earth, the horizon, the beginning of the beginning. Each character told its own story, and when it was combined with one, two, or three others, new stories formed, transforming the initial meaning. And so in this way I followed the series proposed by the book:

言 to speak
   謝 to speak + to bend the body over to greet = to thank
   信 to speak + man = messenger / letter
   說 to speak + to rejoice = to narrate, to say

木 tree
   林 two times tree = bushy, dense
   森 three times tree = severe / dark
   果 fruit + tree = result / full complete

心 heart
   思 heart + brain = reflect

想 heart + to look attentively = to hope / to remember

患 heart + to skewer = unhappiness / to be pained

I had embarked on a race against time. I did not expect to master in six months the minimum of two to three thousand characters required to be able to read a newspaper. But I wanted to prepare myself as best I could to prove myself worthy of Louis and Hà's gift.

As soon as I landed in China, I felt reassured that I could read the signs at the airport for *Exit*, *Baggage*, *Immigration*, and in the street the signs for *Restaurant*, *Bookstore*, and *Hospital*. I had brought along just under a thousand words that I recognized in writing. But I didn't know how to pronounce them, let alone how to put them together into sentences. The kitchen helper at Louis and Hà's residence, A Yi, took me under her wing because I held my two hands out to her to receive a cup of tea with the humility of a child relating to an elder, rather than with the ease of one of her employers' guests; also because I almost choked swallowing the velvety, fibrous pods of edamames; and, most of all, because I answered her with the help of a pencil, tracing characters with the skill of a four-year-old schoolchild. When I wasn't in class, I followed A Yi to the market, to the cleaner's, and, once, to Suzhou, during a three-day holiday.

A YI'S PARENTS still lived in their ancestral home along the canal. My Chinese wasn't good enough for me to ask them questions about their love story in the midst of the Cultural Revolution, beneath images of Mao Zedong, under the one-child policy. But food brought us together, her mother and me, since I was the one who found on the ground the tooth she'd broken while chewing on a ligament from chicken feet sold at the window of the house across the way. The five-spice taste of the feet's marinade was familiar to me, as was the checkerboard with elephants on which A Yi's father played with his son-in-law, next to us.

A Yi's husband came to join us on his return from a trip to France, where he had been an interpreter for a highly placed bureaucrat on a commercial mission. I assumed that he'd studied French because he was a francophile. He politely corrected me, making it clear that he'd become a francophile as a result of studying French. He had been one of the country's best students when he wrote the university entrance exam. The authorities had assigned him to the language department, more specifically, to French. He pronounced his first *bonjour* at the same time as his friends. They never had to ponder nor to choose their profession and their future, because the government had decided for them. If A Yi's husband had been able, he would have chosen agricultural engineering, something that had always been a passion of his. But reasoning with himself, he acknowledged that, in that case, he would not have been one of the privileged individuals authorized and called upon to travel. He would not have slept above the clouds, smelled the conifers on the taiga, witnessed the devotion of the faithful who came to sweep the Shwedagon Pagoda in Rangoon on their birthday. "The State knows you better than you know yourself," he concluded, singing *Je ne regrette rien*.

In my case, it was my brothers, my mother, and Hà who knew me better than I knew myself.

A YI CONFIRMED that the State was beginning to know Louis and Hà very well indeed, since one day she showed them the notebook containing the names of all visitors and the length of their stay at the house. She had to submit it to the city authorities every week. Someone somewhere in a neon-lit office knew that Hà wrote in Vietnamese in her diary when she suddenly awoke during the night, that Louis owned a Rolex watch from the 1940s that he'd inherited from his father, that the couple made significant donations to Tibetan schools . . . On the other hand, I'm sure that he did not hear Louis often declaring at breakfast that he woke up beside the most beautiful woman in the world, nor see him savouring the pleasure he derived from caressing Hà's ebony hair, cut straight across like a Japanese doll's. Louis would have been able to pick out Hà in a crowd just from the shape of her calves. He gazed at her lovingly every time she referred to herself in the Asiatic manner, placing her index finger on the end of her nose instead of against her chest, as Westerners do. I always saw him walking with Hà's hand in his.

Every day, he affixed a new quotation to the bathroom mirror. Hà would invite me to read them with her. Together, we looked for unknown words in the dictionary, and tried to grasp the meaning before Louis returned at the end of the day. "What is your kiss?—The lick of a flame," by Victor Hugo, enabled Hà to teach me the difference between kissing with the mouth in Western culture and with the nose in Vietnamese. While the one tastes, the other smells, which explains the word *thơm* (perfume) for requesting or offering a kiss between young Vietnamese. The quotation "If you loved me and I loved you, how I would love you," by Paul Géraldy, confused tenses. Was the mood wishful or regretful? We did not continue the discussion because Hà reacted very strongly to the word "regret": "Promise me that you will never have any regrets. Never."

AND SO I DID NOT REGRET having pursued my
studies in Quebec rather than in the United States.
Hà pictured me spending my evenings in the library
at Harvard, where Louis had received his degree in
International Relations. He gave us a tour of the university campus, with special emphasis on the library, a
gift from Mrs. Widener in memory of her son who
had died on the *Titanic*. A hundred years later, the
university still places a bouquet of fresh flowers in the
room containing Harry's collection of 3,300 books,
according to his mother's wishes. The library of my
grandfather Lê Văn An probably contained the same
number of books in French and Vietnamese.

As soon as the first Communist tanks rolled into
Saigon, my grandfather ordered us to burn any books
with political content. Over the following weeks, we
also tore up the history books, the novels, and the col-
lections of poetry, in order to eliminate at least one
accusation of treason: possession of anti-revolutionary
instruments. In times of chaos, it's better to be a con-
cierge than a philosopher, a carpenter than a judge.
The police took my grandfather away one afternoon
in the middle of his chess game with Long. He was
released three days later, probably because, as a judge,
he'd been able to free his friends in the resistance. Or
perhaps because the police chief had been touched by
the light of the full moon that cloaked the partially
paralyzed body of my grandfather, stretched out on
the bench under the guava where he had been kept

captive. After his return, the sound of his cane against the tiling underscored the absence of servants, including the one responsible for dusting the books.

If my grandfather had not left us so soon, he would have persuaded my mother to allow me to live in a college dormitory in the United States, even if my opinions on the compulsory course in sexuality in school frightened her. She had signed the authorization while reminding me of the importance of virginity. For a long time, I thought it was my adolescent hormones that had made me reply: "A body is not a thing. So it can't be new or used or second-hand." Time taught me that this way of seeing things came more from Hà and from an article in the *Reader's Digest*, concerning the rapes at sea suffered by boat people.

When I read that, I was fifteen. No boy had even noticed me at the flower table, where I took their dollar in exchange for a Saint Valentine's carnation for the graduates' fundraising campaign. I was as transparent as the petals on the skeleton flower in the rain, even if I was one of the best students in my school. I knew how to disappear so as not to embarrass my friend in front of her companions. Without having given each other clear signs, we knew how to avoid making eye contact when we met in the corridor or the cafeteria. No one suspected that we talked every day on the phone after school hours. I knew about her obsession with knitting, and she, my compulsion for covering each of my books in wrapping paper bought in secret to preserve their status as "presents" all year long. Every dollar I spent on these packages of paper that were "marked-down markdowns," as Marguerite Duras might have said, could have fed a member of my family in Vietnam for three or four days. This was my first selfish act, and also, my first act of love. My books shielded me from my mother's criticisms of my sister-in-law, Hoa. Without them, I would perhaps never have seen the sublime in the blue eyes of Clément, seated at the back of the class with his cheeks as pink as candy apples. They also gave me the courage to refuse the offer of one of my mother's friends to introduce me to "a boy who's somewhat timid," like me.

MY MOTHER KNEW nearly all the mothers, since she worked with the Quebec Association of Vietnamese Women. She often cooked for the New Year's celebration that took place at Complexe Desjardins in Montreal, where all the Vietnamese living in the province converged. In Vietnam, it was very important for my grandparents to see the right person cross the threshold on the first day of the New Year. That person's visit foretold the success or bad fortune that would characterize the year to come. In Quebec, the Vietnamese had abandoned this tradition, because the date of the New Year varied from one year to another between January 21 and February 20, and never fell on a holiday. And so we celebrated Tet on the Sunday preceding the true first day of the lunar year, by meeting in a space vast enough to accommodate the several thousand visitors and, most of all, to set up our food stands.

In contrast to most poor immigrants, we allowed ourselves to spend money with no second-guessing, no feelings of guilt. The restaurants and caterers took in a month's earnings in one day, and the community organizations completed their annual fundraising. The Association of Vietnamese Women probably came out on top, because the fierce but supportive competition among those who wanted to show off their culinary prowess raised the standard of dishes on offer. And so, those Sunday mornings before Tet, Hoa and I woke very early to prepare the herbs, the

thin slices of pork, the shrimp cut lengthwise in two
before being wrapped in rice paper. Even if we were
three people with different hands, all the rolls had to
be the same size, including the three centimetres of
garlic chives that proudly protruded like antennae.
The young people bought those rolls, the stuffed
dumplings, the hot pies, the manioc cake, while the
mothers circulated among the stands to eye the young
unmarried girls a friend or acquaintance had recommended for their sons.

It was during one of these celebrations that a
woman talked to my mother about a boy who lived in
Rimouski. She was of the opinion that he would make
a good husband for me, because our astrological signs
were compatible. "He's not very handsome, but he
works hard, like your daughter, Vi." My mother
wanted a strong man for me, given that I seemed
timid and drab. She smiled politely at the woman.
"Thank you, you're right. But we mustn't make him
come from so far away, the poor boy." In the midst of
the brouhaha, I suddenly heard the word "intrinsic,"
uttered by a young man talking to his friends in the
line in front of our stand. I didn't know that word,
only the sister of the person who had pronounced it.
She was in charge of the cash beside me. I was very
intimidated by how people referred to her as "the
most beautiful young Vietnamese girl." To my great
surprise, she approached me and complimented me on
my straight, dark hair, and on my lashes, thick, but

hidden under the folds of my eyelids. At our first break, she led me into the ladies' washroom to apply mascara that would highlight the true length of my lashes, whose very existence had escaped me until this revelation. She introduced me to her brother, Tân, holding my hand as if we were old friends. I stood there open-mouthed, because Tân's word "intrinsic" had intrigued me, and his smile stole my heart on the spot.

TÂN WAS eight years older than me. By pure chance,
he'd moved from Montreal to Quebec City for his
work and became a close friend of my three brothers,
thanks to badminton. He came to the house so often
that he had his own key, just like the many families
who had lived with us on their arrival in the country.
Never mind the size of our house or of the families,
my mother opened wide our doors to shelter the
FOBs—"fresh off the boats"—for as long as they
wanted. There was so much coming and going that,
once, my brother Loc encountered a thief in the house
and didn't bat an eye, thinking he was someone's
friend. The criminal went off with the car key,
which had been left in plain view, since we shared
everything the same way. Until the police found the
car, Tân politely and generously made his vehicle
available and acted as chauffeur when necessary,
which gave me the opportunity to spend some time
alone with him.

Thanks to my brother Linh, who made a request to
his employer, I was able at the age of sixteen to work
for the same company. I spent my evenings in a huge
empty office printing insurance policies, cheques,
complaints, and other paperwork, which enabled me
to do my homework and study in between feeding
fresh sets of forms into the printer. When there were
no mistakes, I finished around ten o'clock. But the
machines and computer programmes broke down at
the same rhythm as the natural catastrophes or

accidents that befell the insured. When that happened, I missed the last bus. Tân then offered to fetch me, since I was the one who hemmed his new pants and ironed those that had just been washed.

Like my mother with my father, like Hoa with Long, I came to love him slowly, patiently, counting and noting the number of times per week he pronounced my name. I hung his winter coat over the radiator to keep it warm. I refilled his glass with beer so it would stay cold. I placed biscotti beside his coffee to keep alive his adolescence in Rome, the city where his father had lived as a Vietnamese foreign student and, later, as an Italian engineer. Tân introduced us to spaghetti carbonara and therefore to pancetta and parmigiano. He struck up songs in Italian, and imitated Pavarotti. He exposed us to *La Dolce Vita* and all the other films with Marcello Mastroianni. He showed my mother and me the paso doble, the tango, the cha-cha-cha. Santana's "Black Magic Woman" still turns round in my head to the rhythm of his "one, two, cha-cha-cha." For many of the people living in our house, these spontaneous lessons quickly turned into parties where Linh proudly played his cassette mix-tapes.

Those festive days came to an end when Tân's employer called him back to Montreal to work on a new project. His departure gave me the daring idea of following him, of applying to study translation in Montreal universities, of challenging the authority of my mother and brothers. I turned away from their disappointed and uneasy looks. For a long time I had convinced everyone, including myself, that I would become a surgeon, like my first friend in Quebec. She had one day led me to a school library to show me pictures of her dream-to-be. I had not yet acquired the power to dream, so I copied her. I appropriated her ambition, to the point of immortalizing it in my graduation yearbook. There was nothing I had to explain since it pleased everyone and satisfied their expectations. That was why my decision to study translation unnerved my small community. Everyone feared for the precariousness of my future, while they really ought to have worried about my almost total ignorance of the English language and, to a lesser degree, of French. Despite their disapproval, my three brothers slipped money into my pocket the day I moved. At the door to my room in the university residence, my mother said to me, very slowly, in a solemn voice: "When you see that you've made a mistake, I ask you to have the courage to admit it and to start again somewhere else."

I NEVER HAD the courage. I amassed zeros, alone in the half-light of my room. I consoled myself by thinking that at least I was protecting my mother from my failures by keeping my distance from her. Those repeated bad marks reminded me that I ought to continue reading about grammar in my Grevisse, lugging it around in my bag all the time, even if its weight sometimes made me tip over into puddles of water in springtime and onto sheets of ice in winter. Certainly I made progress, leafing through dictionaries, but the difficulties I had day after day persuaded me that I would never be an interpreter for the United Nations in New York, as Hà had hoped. Lacking courage, I persevered through the three years of study, and obtained a degree that I didn't deserve. I see myself again at that time, back bent and head lowered, weighed down by shame as much in the classroom and school corridor as among Tân's family.

My brothers had assigned Tân the task of looking out for me. And so, at least once every two weeks, he invited me for a family dinner at his parents', with whom he still lived. Sometimes he entrusted me to his sisters, who included me in their evenings with other Vietnamese Montrealers. On balconies, around tables, the friends of Tân and his sisters discussed their grades and the specialization they would choose after their studies in medicine, the pharmacies they intended to buy, the dental clinic they would open in one neighbourhood or another still lacking a Vietnamese presence. No one was interested in my story about a brilliant professor who had interpreted a quotation from Shakespeare by citing an equivalent one from Molière, and even less my list of "false friends" between French and English. Does "habit" mean *habitude* in English because men often wear the same *habit*, or suit? How did "bribe" become *pot-de-vin,* a jug of wine, in French? Is *gentillesse* so mild that *gentil* has been transformed into "gentle"? I bored those people with my fascination with disconcerting similarities and differences. But despite the lack of interest on either side, I turned to snag a smile from Tân, to refresh my memory of the sound of his voice, to snare a new movement of his hands.

I WOULD NEVER have obtained my degree in translation without Jacinthe, my classmate from Chibougamou who became a close friend. Jacinthe had been touched by my naiveté when I'd asked the meaning of "rhetoric" and the gender of the word "catastrophe" during an assignment in our first year. She persuaded me to continue my training even though a professor had strongly recommended I switch faculties on account of my disastrous results. I'd never before come last in a class, but I was able to survive the humiliation of my shameful grades thanks to Jacinthe's kindness. She dragged me to boutiques, cafés, and parks, promising to help me complete my assignments at the library on the way back, to make up for lost time. She imposed dance breaks as relief from the long work sessions. Wednesday evenings were reserved for free museum visits. Together, we learned the names of painters, and I absorbed Jacinthe's enthusiasm.

She introduced me to her friends and acquaintances, calling me Lovely Vi, and insisted that Tân respond in the affirmative when she asked, "Isn't she lovely, our Vi?" Tân nodded politely, without sharing her opinion. I imagined him listening to the remarks of his mother: "Vi is tall, but so dark"; "Poor little thing! But at least she's polite." That is why I would never have thought that Tân would kiss me one night in the parking lot behind the Japanese restaurant where I worked every Friday and Saturday. The odours in my hair of grilled eel and sukiyaki mixed with that of tempura made his aftershave intoxicating. He probably only brushed my thighs, but my whole body seemed to have been touched.

I awaited our next meeting, reading the dictionary of synonyms and antonyms, and knitting along with Jacinthe and her roommates. When Tân finally turned up, he offered me a plastic daisy stolen from his mother's floral arrangement instead of a real one. He didn't have to bring any desserts to our private meals in my room because I already had everything he liked in the refrigerator. Even though I didn't drink coffee, he would find a freshly brewed cup every morning he awoke in my bed. He came when it suited him, as I had inserted my key into his key ring even before he expressed a desire to have it.

JACINTHE HAD PERSUADED ME to share an apartment with her on Côte-des-Neiges after we obtained our degrees, so that we could continue studying together, this time in law. Tân spent even more nights with me in the comfort of the nest Jacinthe had created, with its deep-red wall in the living room and the canvases of her painter friends all over. Tân's prolonged and repeated absences made his parents very angry. They summoned me for a lecture on Vietnamese customs and values, concluding with some parental advice: "Think of the gratitude you owe your mother before you keep humiliating her like this."

I hoped that Tân would defend me, defend us, defend himself. To my great surprise, he was also of the opinion that girls from good families did not offer themselves so completely to a man. But out of laziness, ease, comfort, he didn't leave me.

The news had reached my mother's ears through people I had never met. After my first exam in constitutional law, she accosted me outside my apartment. No sooner had she crossed the threshold than my knees were already bent, flat on the floor. She did not take off her coat, because she had only two sentences to say: "I failed in your education. I have just come to look my failure in the face." She left as quickly as she had come, with my brother Lộc, who was waiting in the car. I later found, in the mailbox, an envelope filled with hundred-dollar bills, and a letter from my three brothers, saying: "Come to see us during your reading week, if you can."

I SNUFFED OUT my mother's last spark of hope when I went to join Tân in Berlin to celebrate the fall of the Wall. Tân was there for work during the two months that marked the end of an era, the end of East and West, the end of a long separation. During his absence, I wrote him every day. I received two postcards in response to my letters. One card showed *The Kiss*, by Doisneau. He'd written on the back: "A picture is worth a thousand words." I kept the two with me everywhere I went: on my desk during classes, in my purse when I was out, beside the mirror when I was brushing my teeth. My name had never appeared so precious and so well rendered as it was in Tân's handwriting. When he called me to suggest the trip, I abandoned my family after our Christmas celebrations to fly off to meet him.

In front of the Brandenburg Gate, the Wall was lower and wider, which allowed us to climb on it and watch the crowd converging from both sides. Around us, languages from the four corners of the earth blended into one. The French journalist who lifted us from the ground to help us scramble up offered us the floor of his hotel room if we had no place to sleep. The Portuguese banker who pulled us onto the Wall offered us swigs from his bottle of liquor. A Dutch student shared a chocolate bar with us. I'd been very cold when we visited East Berlin during the day, but the constant greetings and embraces between visitors that evening kept me warm until Tân pulled me out of the arms of a Lebanese man, twice my size, who called us all *habibi*. And so I came down from the Wall, following in the grumpy footsteps of Tân.

My brothers and my mother were not happy to receive the pieces of the Wall I brought back. In their eyes, they were proof of my escapade with Tân, which represented a lack of respect for my ancestors, my culture, and all the struggles and sacrifices of my mother.

IN ORDER TO NORMALIZE the situation and sal-
vage what was left of our reputations, Tân's parents
organized our engagement with my mother. As of
the moment when I prostrated myself before the
altar of the two families' ancestors, we had to call
each other's parents *Ba* and *Má*, "father" and
"mother." It was a given that Hà and Louis would
take a plane from Rio de Janeiro to attend the
engagement ceremony. Hà had insisted on doing my
makeup and setting the traditional headpiece on my
head. While she was taking out the rollers she had
put in to make ringlets, as was the style in her day,
she asked me to promise her I wouldn't marry before
I turned thirty. If I had not received such firm
instructions from Hà, we would certainly have gone
on to make preparations for the wedding, even as Tân
had begun to react badly to my long hours at the law
firm as an intern.

Jacinthe was employed at another big law firm
nearby. There were about twenty of us recruits working very hard, but also going out to eat together, often
at the end of our days, around ten o'clock. Jacinthe
had dozens of admirers. She quickly became known
to the entire legal community. She had an overlapping
canine tooth that gave her a remarkable smile, and her
wild Amazonian hair also made her stand out in a
crowd. She was one of the rare women who dared to
wear Fanta-orange dresses, ivory pantsuits, earrings
that weren't pearls. She wore low-cut tops and

sky-high heels with the natural grace of a woman equally feminist and feminine.

At the first party we held in the apartment, so many colleagues came, along with their friends, that we lost count. Tân was irritated to find strangers asleep in my bed and others entertaining themselves in our bathroom. He left in the middle of the evening with a comment that marked the beginning of the end of our relationship: "You 'work' with these people?"

As of that euphoric night amidst young people whose philosophy was *work hard*, *play harder*, Tân was no longer satisfied with the stews I cooked, or with the spaghettini with lemon zest, or the meat pies from Jacinthe's parents. One evening he was so indignant to learn that I would not attend the upcoming anniversary of his great-grandfather's death because of a company weekend retreat that he threw in the garbage the croque monsieur I'd prepared for him, plate and all. Jacinthe sprang from her chair like a lioness and chased Tân away. If I hadn't begged her with a frightened and shamefaced look, she probably would have slapped him, in addition to shouting in her serious and powerful voice: "You don't deserve her. Get out!"

It took several weeks before I mustered up the courage to call Tân's parents and ask them for a brief meeting. They insisted that their son be present. I brought them the earrings and necklace they had given me when we became engaged, as well as the diamond ring that Tân, in my presence, had bought at the last minute from an acquaintance of his mother, in full confidence and without having even looked at it.

There was neither a box, nor an entreaty, nor promises. I had to consider myself privileged that Tân's parents had accepted me as a daughter-in-law despite my shortcomings. I apologized to them for my mother's absence. But as parents, they understood that I wanted to spare her this moment of dishonour. Tân's mother concluded that my disobedience was responsible for the drama. I ought to have followed her advice and been friends only with those in Tân's circle. He shut tight the door, mumbling that he'd known since the very start, as soon as I'd yielded to his first kiss in the automobile, that I was too Western.

My behaviour had ruined the reputations of two perfectly respectable families. My mother had to answer questions from curious mothers and, worst of all, put up with their murderous remarks: "Letting her live alone was a mistake"; "Hà had a bad influence on Vi"; "What boy will want her now?" . . .

I broke away from my mother. I broke my mother. As my father had broken her.

I WOULD HAVE been broken myself had it not been for one of the lawyers in the office, a president of the Bar, who invited me to travel with her to Cambodia for a meeting with colleagues from Phnom Penh, Hanoi, and Luang Prabang. We discussed the writing of their civil code, the influence of French law after and without colonialism, the disappearance of the ideological frontier between East and West, between Communism and capitalism, and so on. The foreign experts in shirts and ties presented their analyses, making no reference to the bullet holes in the outside walls—and sometimes even inside, such as one that could be seen below the blackboard. While we emphasized the importance of judicial independence, a nine-year-old boy who walked every day from his village an hour from Phnom Penh to a school beside our meeting room copied every page of the English–Khmer / Khmer–English dictionary into his notebook, because his village had no books, and certainly no judge. If we ignored the amputees and the weapons resting on restaurant tables, it was easy to imagine the "Pearl of Asia" that Phnom Penh had been, with its sumptuous temples and villas. But all it took was a visit to the temples of Siem Reap, where you stumbled over the head of a Buddha, plundered and abandoned by a looter, to hear the footsteps of those marching towards death under the regime of Pol Pot.

The image of skulls piled up by the hundreds, of children held by their feet and flung against the

CAMBODIA
KÂMPŬCHEA
~
land of Khmers

trunks of trees, became somewhat easier to process after my one-day visit to Siem Reap. In one of the Angkor temples, an old woman in a sarong pulled me by the hand to a corner bathed in light, where she delivered blows to my chest. The echo of ancient stones spread through my rib cage, and brought my life's breath back to me. Thanks to the imprint of this bony hand on my skin, I dared to sit down and offer a pink satin ribbon retrieved from the bottom of my purse to the little girl who sold water and ant eggs to the tourists. While the sun was going down and I was wondering how to leave this young merchant to her futureless tomorrow, a group of three men passed before us. One of them was explaining in French to the other two that the city of Angkor covered a territory greater than that of Paris today and that you must not confuse the *devatas*, who served as guardians, with the *apsaras*, dancers able to seduce both men and gods. I wondered if the Communist inspector who had characterized my father's two precious apsara sculptures as "cultural corruption" knew the difference. Perhaps he had confiscated them because he was already taken with them, as I suddenly was by the third man in the group, who spent a long time trailing the ends of his fingers along the walls, following the curve of the apsaras' smooth and provocative hands, open to what lay beyond.

I flew back to Montreal the next day, with a clear and indelible picture of the back of that stranger's neck and the arc of his shoulder. I never imagined that one day I would fall asleep in the hollow of that very neck.

ON MY RETURN, a fellow lawyer called me into his
office to talk about a long-term aid project on political reform in Vietnam. Since he was known to be
one of the most brilliant men in the country, I agreed
unconditionally, not knowing that Vietnamese-
Americans who dared to travel to Vietnam sometimes
saw their houses vandalized, and that Vietnamese-
Canadians demonstrated in front of Parliament
against the resumption of diplomatic relations
between the two countries. I boarded the plane totally
ignorant of the highly sensitive and purely political
nature of the project.

Before finding a permanent office, we established
our headquarters in the small hotel where our team
was lodged. During the day, our rooms became our
offices, and the restaurant, our boardroom. We ate
breakfast, lunch, and dinner together. We closed our
doors late in the evening, at the same time.

As for me, I spent a good part of the night search-
ing through dictionaries of English–French / French–
English / English–Vietnamese / Vietnamese–English
/ French–Vietnamese / Vietnamese–French, as well
as unilingual dictionaries, because the word "soft-
ware" did not exist in Vietnam during the 1970s,
any more than "environment" or "ASEAN." The
Vietnamese language I knew was marked by exile
and trapped in an antiquated reality, one that pre-
ceded the Soviet presence and the strong ties with
Cuba, Bulgaria, Czechoslovakia, Romania . . . More

than thirty thousand Vietnamese live in Warsaw, and in Berlin the Vietnamese quarter is much larger than Montreal's Chinatown. The history of Vietnam and the Vietnamese endures, evolves, and grows in complexity without being written down or told.

I TRIED TO seek out some fragments of Vietnam's
twenty years behind the Iron Curtain by hanging
around restaurant tables. Across from my hotel, there
were several. One offered *bánh mì* sandwiches, another
sautéed vermicelli, and many served Tonkinese soup,
or pho. I ended my days with this soup, which in no
way resembled that served in Montreal, Los Angeles,
Sydney, or Saigon. The Hanoi version was sold with
only a few slices of rare beef, while I had always
eaten this dish with a dozen ingredients, including
tendons, stomach, shank, Thai basil, and bean
sprouts. People from the south of Vietnam love
making fun of the economical and less extravagant
mindset of those in the North, using the example of
how many items constitute "a dozen." In the North,
the dozen represents ten units; in the centre-North,
twelve; in the centre-South, fourteen; and in the
Mekong, sixteen and sometimes eighteen.

At first, I found very bland the pho made by the
restaurant owner-cook on the sidewalk in front of my
hotel. In time, I came to appreciate the simplicity that
allowed me to taste the kaffir lime leaf in the chicken
version, and the grilled ginger in the one made with
beef. Obviously, I had to beg the woman not to season
my bowl with a spoonful of monosodium glutamate,
an ingredient that was precious during the war.
During the difficult years, that salt was not used just
to enhance flavour; it was the flavour itself, the only
ingredient added to white rice. Out of habit, my

restaurant owner-cook continued to rely on this product to round out the flavours, even though her soup now contained real chicken and even though meat was no longer rationed. However, some old reflexes helped her to follow the rhythm of the police raids. Their duty was to temporarily chase away people illegally occupying the public thoroughfare, but only on one sidewalk at a time. That allowed my cook and her husband to ask their four or five clients to get up with their bowls before they moved the table to the other side of the street. The police check lasted only a few minutes, and the neighbours had enough advance notice for the sellers to simply cross the street. Once, I finished my soup under a tree while marvelling at this perfectly synchronized choreography.

DURING THE FIRST MONTHS of my posting to
Hanoi, I was as fascinated by the ability of a young
child to sit on her father's bicycle carrier without
catching her feet in the spokes as by the drivers asleep
on the seats of their moto-taxis. And even more by the
six versions of the word "adore" in Vietnamese: to
adore madly; to adore to the point of going rigid as a
tree; to adore giddily; to adore to the point of losing
consciousness; to the point of fatigue; to the point of
losing one's grip on oneself. I wanted to see everything, learn everything.

Both our office and my apartment were situated on
the peninsula in the Trúc Bạch neighbourhood that
was reputed to produce the finest bells and bronze
statues. We chose the location for the discretion of
both the place and its inhabitants, who had inherited
the austerity of the ancient prison built by an
eighteenth-century noble to incarcerate his concubines
whom he suspected of criminal activity. I was happy
to be out of the way so as not to have to refuse for the
tenth time in one morning a lottery ticket sold by war
amputees; so as not to hear the conversations between
expatriates about the roughness of the talc used by the
masseuses for a hand job; so as not to be enraged
when the indecently luxurious cars of the new mil-
lionaires passed by the five- or six-year-old shoeshine
kids. Above all, I avoided the prettiest café in Hanoi,
on the shore of the Lake of the Restored Sword,
because I felt personally hurt by the rude remark of a

foreign client about a waiter who didn't know the difference between a macchiato and a cappuccino. Each time, I died a little from my cowardice in not defending these young boys who probably slept in their booths after closing and, most of all, who didn't have the good fortune even to taste one of those coffees. On the other hand, I felt responsible for the hugely inflated prices charged to visitors, and sometimes for the rudeness the Vietnamese allowed themselves when they thought they were protected by the language barrier.

I distanced myself from these discomforts and confused feelings by concentrating on my work. It was much easier to analyze a state-owned corporation on paper than to meet the employees who lived on the company property with their families. Similarly, organizing a seminar on the subject of citizen protection in the person of an ombudsman seemed less futile when I did not see the envelopes slipped into the files of highly placed bureaucrats to "contribute to their children's education."

MY SIXTY-EIGHT-YEAR-OLD BOSS WAS the youngest man in my circle in Hanoi. He watched over me like a father, and urged me to accept invitations to various events. Often, the burden of my work enabled me to decline, with the exception of the July 14 celebration at the French embassy, as it was important for me to be there in support of the French-speaking world. Respecting protocol, I greeted a few people, who replied courteously without taking much of my time. And so it was easy for me to disappear behind the bronze sculpture of two storks at the back of the garden, in order to escape the conversation about the maid who had ironed a pleated skirt, "a collector's item designed by Issey Miyake"; or about the restoration of a mahogany table with a mother-of-pearl centre that had been left out in the sun and the rain; or about the list of the first state corporations selected for the imminent arrival of the stock market in Vietnam.

Vincent approached me, asking if I knew the difference between storks and cranes. "Storks clack their beaks but don't sing, unlike cranes, who can cry very loudly while making love."

We left the embassy garden when the waiters began folding the chairs. Vincent took me back on his old Chinese bicycle, and I sat in front of him on the cross-bar. He took the route that went past the former house of the governor of Indochina, where the milkwood pine's flowers perfumed the entire neighbourhood.

The next day, he came to fetch me for breakfast at the elegant Mme Simone Đài's, where crepes were served with sugar and lime juice, along with homemade yogurt and croissants, called "buffalo horns" by the waiters. At lunchtime, he introduced me to peanuts roasted in fish sauce, which the "locals" ate with rice. In the evening, I pedalled at his side to Hồ Tây, where young lovers shared snails cooked in medicinal herbs. In less than twenty-four hours I saw that Hanoi was much more than the fifteen streets and six addresses that I frequented from day to day.

In the space of just a few days, Vincent had offered me the world, explaining the behaviour of the female anopheles mosquito that transmitted malaria; the recent discovery of a new species of bird at the very heart of Phnom Penh; the existence of the baculum bone in the male genital organ of almost all primates with the exception of man . . . I hadn't known that the discipline of ecologist-ornithologist existed, nor that it was possible to find undocumented birds within the territory of Vietnam. He had succeeded in persuading the government to establish protected zones after many years of concentrated and patient work, mingling with the people, learning the minority ethnic languages, amassing an intimate knowledge of the forests, some of which had begun to come back to life after the Agent Orange bombings, the fires, the tears of the children.

A VIETNAMESE MOTHER in exile had for a long time wandered through the Norwegian forests to withstand the absence of her son lost in another forest, in Vietnam, during their flight from guns, bombs, cataclysm. As soon as she had been able to return to her original forest, she had continued her search, and thanks to the birthmark on his left ear she had recognized her son, who had become a chicken seller. A Cham family had found the child on the lifeless body of his father, and had undone the band of cloth that had enabled the man to carry him. The baby certainly must have cried when his father fell. But how could the mother, who was running through the smoke after her older daughter, distinguish her son's tears in the midst of all the others? Perhaps, too, the baby had awakened only after the chaos, like Jacinthe's father, who slept in front of the television set and awoke when his wife switched it off. Vincent knew only that the baby, now a father, asked him to explain to his biological mother that he wanted to stay near his wife and three children on the land of his adoptive parents, even if he ran the risk of being mistreated as a "native."

The blood of the mountain people flowed in his veins. He owed his loyalty to the Cham culture and was determined to defend that language, which was in the process of disappearing. Vincent devoted himself to this group as much as to the populations of redheaded cranes and laughingthrushes, because he had

made it his profession to protect the vulnerable. When
he showed me the reaction of the *mimosa pudica*
leaves, which closed up at the gentlest touch to protect
themselves from predators, he convinced me that I
was wrong to believe I was as invisible and common
as the grass that grew between cracks in the cement
without attracting the attention of anyone besides shy
young girls. He compared me to the rare *udumbara*
flowers, which the Buddhists said appeared only once
every three thousand years, whereas in fact they hid
by the hundreds beneath the skin of their fruits.
Sometimes they escaped to blossom on a leaf, on a
wire fence, or in my entire body after our first kiss.

WHILE I LIVED in a space as empty as the echo that circulated there in response to a rare noise, in Vincent's home every object spoke and told its story. They came from different places, different times, different cultures, but were melded, woven together like a nest. The long cushion set on a wooden bench with the finely carved back was filled with kapok gathered, worked, and sold by an Indonesian family with whom he had stayed; the teapot hidden in a coconut whose interior had been shaped to fit the curve of the ceramic pot and retain the water's heat belonged to the monk who had lived in this "hut" before him; the cutting board came from the trunk of a hundred-year-old tree fallen during combat, which Vincent had helped to move. In the garden he had hung up, in the form of a cross, two enormous stalks of bamboo, on which he had suspended a dozen cages that had imprisoned the rare birds he had bought from collectors in order to return them to their natural habitats.

In the evening, a woman he called his "Vietnamese mother" lit candles inside the cages to illuminate the garden before going back home. I saw in her wrinkled eyes that I was not the first woman to marvel at the starfruit, to be bewitched by the perfume of the yellow-hearted white flowers of the frangipani, and to fall in love with the rice-husk colour of the loose curls at the nape of Vincent's neck. He heated water in two enormous kettles to fill a cement reservoir for gathering rainwater, which he had transformed into a bathtub.

It was in this bath, constantly rewarmed with water from the kettles, that he asked me to go with him to London for a fundraising event where he would put up for auction the naming rights to his next discovery. He knew from experience that people are prepared to spend tens of thousands of dollars, even hundreds of thousands, to immortalize their passage on earth.

IN THE WHISPERING GALLERY of St. Paul's Cathedral, Vincent's voice travelled across and set its stamp on the thirty-four metres of wall separating us, uttering two of the most time-worn words in the French language, but words that had never been addressed to me. Before I could reply, he'd already taken my hand to run to the British Library, where he showed me the Magna Carta, the manuscript of *Alice in Wonderland*, and the first book ever printed. He was as at ease in a T-shirt as in the tuxedo with cufflinks he wore to present before a packed hall his birds and their story. He took his audience on a journey, describing the life of the forest, as if every tree had its own personality, and every animal a destiny, and that together they lived in harmony, as enemies, as lovers . . . He ended his slide show with the photo of a giant flower, twice his height, which bloomed only once every ten years, for only seventy-two hours. He provoked a burst of laughter and applause in concluding that men, being what they are, had called it "Titan's phallus." He had to hold me by the waist so as not to lose me in the crush of women who saw in him the reincarnation of Tarzan, with his handsome face, his jade eyes, and his protective shoulders. Over and over, he introduced me with the same words used by Jacinthe: "Please meet my lovely Vi"; "*Je vous présente ma belle Vi*"; "*Darf ich Ihnen meine wundervolle Freundin Vi vorstellen?*"

DURING OUR CAR TRIP to the Cornwall coast to sleep at the mythic Headland Hotel at Newquay, I asked him why. Why me? He said that he'd seen me braiding the hair of the little girl who sold ant eggs three years earlier in Cambodia. He'd expected to find me that evening at the Grand Hôtel d'Angkor restaurant, where almost all the foreigners converged, but he'd looked for me in vain. As usual, from fear, from timidity, from ignorance, I'd preferred to eat alone in my hotel room with a book.

Life gave us a second chance much later, in Hanoi. Vincent had glimpsed me through the half-open door to the room he had just left, where the first meeting between my boss and the minister of the environment took place. He could tell that I'd been settled in the capital for only a short time since, in contrast to the powder blue or sky blue of Vietnamese silk, the royal blue of my dress still evoked the bold colour of the French flag. As well, my pink cheeks betrayed my rapid Western gait and my ignorance of the slow pace of a country in the process of change. He would have liked to reach me right after he had learned the location of my office from the assistant to the minister of the environment. Unfortunately, along with other colleagues, he had to leave for an extended period of time to explore a recently discovered grotto. He interpreted this third chance encounter at the embassy as a sign.

In the forest, amid dozens of animals of all sorts that appeared and disappeared around him, the colour of a feather, the length of a beak, the form of a nest, would catch his eye and reveal to him the features of a species. As for what had captivated him about me, it was my ability to bend my legs, to curve my back, and to hunch my shoulders to match the fragility of the young merchant who was preparing portions of ant eggs with the help of small green leaves.

WHEN WE CAME BACK FROM England, Vincent continued his excursions into the forest. His extended absences made me doubt the true existence of the evenings spent at his side, jumping when an acrobatic rat dropped into the wok of the vendor of sautéed crab vermicelli; watching a dragonfly land on his mortar's pestle while he was grinding up a mixture of spices; going to sleep under the mosquito netting whose four corners were attached with threads of different colours, rolled around rusted nails hammered crookedly into different walls and beams. Had I not received every morning from the hand of a messenger the photo of a bird with its description, along with a photo of a part of me, I would have thought that I had dreamed my life or created a mythic character to provide me with a dream life.

Vincent reminded me not to sit sidesaddle on moto-taxis if the driver seemed drunk; not to buy meat from the merchant who chased away flies by spraying his strips of pork with Raid; not to leave anti-mosquito spirals lit while I slept; not to exchange dollars for dongs on street corners; not to eat the same woman's pho every night . . . On the other hand, he forgot to warn me that the Red River overflowed its banks during harvest season. The water rose in only a few hours, forcing the people living beside it to save their refrigerators on little aluminum boats built by artisans in the next neighbourhood. They dove into the water to unplug the television or to lift up a piece of

furniture. Without the earthen dyke surrounding
Hanoi, the city would have been submerged long ago.
That dyke had survived a number of wars, but I wondered if it would support the new construction on its
back for much longer. For that reason, one day the
authorities cut off the houses that extended beyond
the limits of the dyke, leaving a surreal landscape of
open living rooms, split kitchens, amputated bed-
rooms with their residents continuing to live there as
if onstage, in a play. I lived a few streets from the
dyke. I was certain that the wooden beams blocking
its openings would give way under the pressure of
water and chaos. From my balcony on the sixth floor,
I made a list of the dozens of ways to die, and electro-
cution easily came out on top, since hundreds of tan-
gled electrical wires were suspended in a disorderly
and precarious manner all over the streets. Lightning
frightened me, because I had to go out on the balcony
to empty the water that flowed freely into the apartment, cascading down the six floors of steps inside
the building.

That night, I would have liked to have a god to
whom I could entrust Vincent. I also wanted to call
my mother to apologize for having always disappointed
her. On my last visit, she died a little whenever I pronounced Vietnamese words newly acquired in the
North, with a Northern accent. Her friends lamented
the fact that she had raised a daughter who'd gone
back to serve Communism, that I had become a red

princess, a traitor to the memory of the Southern soldiers. If I were to be struck by lightning, I wanted her to know that I had met mothers who had not chosen to send their sons to the front, who had not chosen their political allegiance, who had only hoped that their children would survive them, just like her. But I did not call her. Because I would have worried her with my fear in the middle of the storm.

Vincent cut short his expedition when he heard about the torrential rains. He forced me to come to him, because my mattress was still damp on account of the water leaking from the roof. The hundred-year-old tiles of his little house seemed to drain away water more effectively than recent constructions, modelled on Soviet architecture. I took shelter in his arms, tucking my head into the hollow of his collarbone as if the storm were still rumbling away behind the shutters. Every time I opened my eyes that night, Vincent's gaze met mine as if he had not slept, as if I were one of his birds, which he observed with kindness and patience. "Tell me about the storm, my angel."

I TOLD Vincent how I'd transported the little
refrigerator from the ground-floor office to the first
floor, how I'd pulled the mattress in front of the balcony to block the water coming in under the door,
how I'd resorted to repeating the Sanskrit mantra that
my Buddhist grandmother had taught me.

I also told him how Monsieur Luân, a highly
placed official, had left his mark by licking my ear at
the end of our meeting in my office. Had I not heard
Hà's voice in my head, I would have frozen like a
fawn in the headlights instead of reflexively walking
to the door and leaving. Hà often told me that it was
not my buttons done up to the neck and at the wrists
that would protect me, but the strength I would draw
on to disengage myself.

Whispering Hà's words into the hollow of Vincent's
collarbone, I realized that my mother had taught me
above all to become as invisible as possible, or at least
to transform myself into a shadow so that no one
would attack me, to pass through walls and melt into
my surroundings. She insisted that in the art of war,
the first lesson consisted of mastering one's disappearance, which was at the same time the best attack and
the best defence. Until I saw the light shining like
crystals in Vincent's beads of perspiration, I had
always thought that my mother preferred her boys out
of habit, out of love for my father. My voice echoing in
the circle of Vincent's arms finally led me to under-
stand my mother's desire to have me grow up

differently, to launch myself elsewhere, to offer myself a fate different from her own. It took me two continents and an ocean to grasp that she had had to go against her nature to entrust the education of her own daughter to Hà, another woman, far away from her, and her exact opposite.

I HAD NEVER been at all curious about visiting
Burma before the day Vincent awaited me at the
Rangoon airport for the weekend of the Water
Festival and the Buddhist New Year. He'd been
working in that country for some time, trying to con-
vince the government of the purely scientific nature of
his organization, whose sole objective was to protect
the environment in regions at risk. His organization
functioned the way birds do, paying no heed to fron-
tiers and migrating from one region to another,
unconcerned about the political regime in power. In
Burma, the military junta imposed absolute obedience
on the populace, to the letter, with an exception made
for automobiles, which were permitted to have the
steering wheel on the left or on the right. The leader
in power set great store by the advice of astrologers,
who recommended changing the direction of traffic in
the streets in the name of the country's security, even
if the public buses opened their doors on the opposite
side. The collective good had to trump the individual
good where peace and order were concerned.

Fortunately, Bagan seemed to have been protected
from the leaders' mood swings. Perhaps its three thousand temples safeguarded it from the course of time
and the uneasiness of the people seated uncomfortably
on the pointed summits of the pyramids. Vincent
wrapped me in the cocoon of this city, where everything seemed to move to the rhythm of the wagons
pulled by daydreaming mules. To celebrate the start of

the Burmese new year, tradition decreed that people be cleansed of their sins of the past year by sprays of perfumed water. In Bagan, you used the palms of your hands rather than pumps and cannons with powerful jets, as in Bangkok or Rangoon. We bought sarongs at the market, and also a length of bark from a nutmeg tree, whose yellow powder protected the skin from the burning sun. Men slathered their faces with it, while women drew circles on their cheeks out of simple vanity. Vincent drew dozens of patterns on me, while I in turn applied this powder to his arms, his legs, and his back, writing a thousand words of love with my finger. He took hundreds of photographs of us, for our future children.

BAGAN'S SLOWNESS called to mind that of
Cairanne, in France, where Vincent's family had a
second home surrounded by vineyards. Vincent
wanted to plan a visit to our respective families in
Quebec and Cairanne, one after the other, during the
Christmas break at the end of the year. I had told only
Hà that I'd found my "Louis," that I'd become the
woman she'd always dreamed I would be, that I now
saw life from a lookout on its dizzying heights. I was
gliding on the wings of Vincent's birds. He himself
had helped me to grow my own wings, by calling me
"my angel" and by orchestrating flights for me: by
airplane, by parachute, by hot-air balloon.

I no longer feared that my mother would stop
speaking French to show that she disapproved of
Vincent. I only wanted to share with her this sudden
lust for life that I was experiencing for the first
time, but circumstances didn't give me that opportunity. She suffered a mild heart attack that con-
fined her to a hospital bed one week before the date
planned for my visit to Quebec. I stayed near her at
my brother Long's during her convalescence, which
made it impossible for Vincent to come, and for me
to go to Cairanne.

Hoa had given birth to the first baby in our family
a year earlier. My mother would have liked her
grandson to bear the complete name of her sole and
eternal love, Lê Văn An. My brother had kept only
the "Lê," contending that our father had forfeited

this privilege the day he'd allowed his wife and children to struggle on alone. Long would have liked his father to have witnessed the success of his restaurant business and his many honours for innovation and leadership. And that he should feel regret for having been absent. Long's rapid rise had frightened my mother, who remembered what her father had said when she became Đa Lạt's major producer of orchids: "Success often brings unhappiness." She still blamed herself for having worked too hard and, above all, for having loved too intensely. If she had denied her husband his escapades, if she had allowed him to come to her instead of constantly anticipating his desires, if she had wept to his face and not in hiding, perhaps he would have been able to assume his role as head of the family. She had tried to compensate by strengthening Hoa's ability to offer Long a haven of absolute calm and serenity after his turbulent days of meetings and of women who took too much interest in him. On the other hand, she often insisted on taking the baby so Hoa could go to the hairdresser regularly, exercise every day, and accompany Long to social events. Living in one of the two parts of the bi-generational house designed by Long, she could easily withdraw and involve herself according to what was required. She monitored Long's homecomings. If he arrived too late too often, she prepared his favourite dishes. She called him at work without making demands, without mentioning that a family was waiting for him, without reminding him that he should resist his desires. She simply brought the dishes to Hoa, and hoped to hear a laugh or two through the walls.

AS FOR LỘC, my mother rarely visited him. He had
stayed to work at Princeton after his post-doctorate in
oncology. She could not resist noting with sadness
that his American wife fed him mostly frozen food.
Lộc cooked better and much more often than Sheryl
did. My mother understood that they took pleasure in
discussing molecules and collaborating on one article
or another. To her mind, their conjugal partnership
enhanced their professional relationship and vice versa.
But she kept her opinions to herself, out of respect,
and largely because of a lack of understanding. She
contented herself with filling the trunk of Lộc's car
with prepared dishes, preserved in coolers. Out of love,
Lộc carried it all off and, at the border, lied when the
customs agent asked him if he had any food.

SHERYL TURNED OUT to be a perfect daughter-in-law compared with Linh's Taiwanese wife. Mei was so pretty that the Chinese restaurants in Montreal always placed her at their entrances, as a hostess. Linh fell in love with her the first time they met, and moved to Montreal as soon as he could. They seemed to be living a perfect love, even if Mei finished working in the early morning hours, long after the restaurants closed. Linh never complained about waiting for her to come home at night since he used the time to work on his consultant contracts in addition to his daytime job.

At their wedding, I'd heard guests sharing under their breath the Vietnamese saying: "A beautiful wife belongs to others." In Linh's case, his wife was swallowed up by gambling; Linh was replaced by the casino. In only a few years, she lost her youthful air, her innocence, and the house they owned. Despite his well-paying jobs, Linh had to give up on the marriage. My mother had never allowed herself to lament her break with my father, but she surrendered to Linh's sadness. Perhaps Linh's pain stretched her fighting spirit to the breaking point. When I saw her facial muscles sag after what happened, the image that came to my mind was the English expression *the straw that broke the camel's back*. Since then, I've looked for an equivalent in French. I'm often advised that it's *la goutte qui fait déborder le vase*, "the drop that makes the bowl overflow." But that expression does not do justice to my mother's collapse. She withdrew and turned in on herself as if she had been broken. Fortunately, her grandson was born, which gave her a reason to pull herself together.

MY MOTHER MADE ME return to Hanoi, promising me, hollowly, that she would come to visit me as soon as Long completed the acquisition of a new franchise. Hoa took me to the airport, and comforted me with the news that they were expecting a second child. "That will put her back on her feet. Don't worry."

As usual, I'd boarded the plane with a suitcase full of books. At the time, only photocopies of photocopies of *The Lover,* by Marguerite Duras, of *The Quiet American*, and of some Lonely Planet guides were being sold in the street by illiterate youngsters in rags. Sometimes, two or three Hanoi bookstores offered copies of college books left behind by expatriates. Overwhelmed as I was by all aspects of the project I was working on, I tried to read what was available so I'd be able to participate, without being too anxious, in meetings with the directors of state corporations, farmers, the National Assembly's Committee on Social Affairs. Those readings also enabled me to not count Vincent's days of absence minute by minute.

After the Christmas holidays, Vincent landed in Hanoi two days after me. I prepared us a Vietnamese fondue that evening, with a clear bouillon in which we cooked slices of chicken, beef, and pork, as well as clams and shrimp. Vincent's favourite part was the basket of greens that accompanied the meats. His "Vietnamese mother" had helped me to find the water lily rhizomes, the young bamboo shoots, the water spinach, the banana flowers, the squash blossoms, the

okra, the straw mushrooms . . . and a kind of shy
mimosa with a taste and texture he particularly liked.
This dish was tastier if it was eaten in a group,
because the bouillon was richer when a large quantity
of ingredients was involved. And so, even though I
would have preferred to keep Vincent all to myself, I
shared him with our friends who were in Hanoi. The
ephemeral but intense friendship with expatriates
made for a very special family. Since movies, theatre,
and any other cultural activity did not exist in foreign
languages, we had to provide our own entertainment.

Sundays, we would spend three or four hours at a
huge brunch at the Sofitel Hotel, which offered an
oasis of food not to be found on the local market:
rosettes de Lyon, knuckle of ham, *blanquette de veau*,
brioches, gravlax, crèmes brûlées, oysters, cassoulet,
coq au vin, *baba au rhum*, sautéed foie gras, langoust-
ines, *Paris-Brests*, *tarte Tatin*, a platter with a thousand
cheeses . . . On other days of the week, we often circulated from one home to another, to treat our
friends to our discoveries. Drew, an Australian who
divided his time between India and Vietnam, introduced us to Indian spices; Antoine, who was
Lebanese and a true gourmet, knew how to grill fish
to perfection; Marianne, a Brazilian from Rio, prepared more cocktails than food; Philipp, a German,
was always prompt, even in a country where time was
an elastic concept; Nicholas, our big polar bear, did
everything with love. Around the table, we often

matched the number of member nations of the United Nations Security Council, representing many different disciplines, and with hundreds of stories to tell.

The night of the fondue, Vincent politely shooed away our guests earlier than usual, because he wanted us to open our Christmas presents alone together. For several months he had been growing winter heather in the mountains because he'd heard me comment at length on the thicket of heather in a photo of their house, rather than marvelling at their ancestral dwelling at Orléans in the background. After several attempts, he succeeded in filling a jardinière that fit perfectly on the windowsill. My second present was a bag of white-fleshed cherries, a fruit that was out of season but as delicious as the red ones of autumn. During my childhood in Vietnam, we all drew cherries in the same way, attached by their stalks, even though none of us had ever seen, let alone tasted, one. There was a kind of fruit with the same name, *sơ ri*, but it didn't have anything like the same features. One was big, the other little; one sweet, the other acid. The most remarkable difference concerned the pit. The Vietnamese *sơ ri* contained three soft pits, whereas the other possessed only one hard one. Vincent's cherry enabled me to keep for myself the half containing the pit when we bit into it at the same time. But immediately he put his index finger on my lips while kissing my temple. I was astonished that he noticed, because I don't think my father ever knew that my mother took the seeds out of his bananas and cucumber slices before serving them to him. Similarly, Tân certainly thought that his wallet attracted his keys thanks to an invisible magnet, just as his jackets automatically took their places on their hangers. Despite the coffee that dripped through the filter while he was taking his shower, and the carefully shined shoes that awaited him beside the door, he was blinded by the grey sky, the cry of a neighbour's alarm clock, the hike in income tax and sales tax.

I could have cut off ten centimetres of my hair and Tân wouldn't have noticed, whereas the least sign of a burn immediately attracted the attention and care of Vincent. He had had "Vi" tattooed above his right hip, at the level of his belt, a mark that presaged my third present: a ring adorned with a square sapphire and diamond chips on all four sides. It had belonged to his grandmother, who had taken it straight from her little finger the day after their Christmas Eve celebration. Vincent had shown her photos of me. From her large collection of jewels she had chosen to leave her favourite grandson this first ring given her long ago by her jeweller husband.

Vincent's sapphire touched and overwhelmed me, as I had lost my four grandparents, and had not tried to see my father again since my return to Vietnam. My story had been cut short, reinvented. No object of my mother's or mine spoke of the generations, unlike the altar of ancestors that bore witness to all marriages, anniversaries of deaths, of New Year's ceremonies going back at least a hundred years. Had this piece of furniture become the focal point of another family since it had been taken away from us? Had the souls of my ancestors followed it or had they stayed with my father? Or had they also fled along with us in order to bring us to safe harbour? The sapphire ring that I wore on my finger bound me to Vincent's love, but most of all it included me in the long history of his great family, even if that history was still unknown to me, and remains so.

I WAS RESPONSIBLE for a mission to Singapore with a group of Vietnamese advisers when Vincent received the news about his grandmother's serious condition after a banal fall. He got the first plane out to join his entire family and to be with the woman who had taught him to play his first notes on the piano, to recite his first poem, to knot his first bow tie. In his olfactory memory, no perfume was as sweet and comforting as that of the jam made from melons gorging with honey that she served warm with Brillat-Savarin cheese melting in the afternoon sun. The photo of bouquets of lavender hanging from the beam over her kitchen helped me imagine the young Vincent carrying a wicker basket and following his grandmother into the fields. He adored the woman who had provided him with his French roots despite a life as the son of a diplomat, changing countries and friends to the rhythm of elections, and living in borrowed shells, like a hermit crab.

We had no way to communicate during my mission to Singapore because of the six time zones that separated us and my heavy schedule. When I returned, Vincent called me, his voice muffled by sadness and fatigue. During his second telephone call he was more optimistic, as his grandmother had begun to eat a few mouthfuls of applesauce. The danger was over, which allowed him to anticipate returning to Hanoi. And then— nothing. No more news, other than a note I received two weeks after his last call: "My love, I miss you."

Vincent's "Vietnamese mother" was also in the dark, with no news from him. But she was used to his absences and his unpredictable returns. She continued to take care of the house, gathering up yellow leaves and faded petals, dusting the shutters and his bicycle, replacing the fruits in the basket in case he returned during the night. I asked her not to change the sheets or wash Vincent's clothes, which I slept with. She consoled me with congee and ginger tea. No one had any news, not even his colleagues. His organization's headquarters in London had no contact information other than that for Vietnam, since he'd already been living there for seven years.

I MOVED into Vincent's little house. His "Vietnamese mother" and I did our best to move nothing around, to alter nothing. I saved every one of his hairs found in the dust, in the matting, in the hammock's mesh. His sandals and slippers I wrapped in tissue paper so the imprints of his feet would remain intact. I bought the same candles, the same detergent, the same shampoo. In that way, when I arrive at the house, I plunge into the same ambient scents. I did not keep the same circle of friends, though, because it became hard to avoid discussing theories regarding his disappearance. In any case, those people change cities and countries frequently, depending on their postings and contracts, always of uncertain duration.

My two constant ones, Hà and Jacinthe, took turns coming to visit me. Jacinthe brought me photos of my mother and her grandchildren. Hà gave me one of the diamond earrings my mother had received at the time of her wedding. She had swallowed both of them to pass through the anti-capitalist body search in Saigon, and had found only one three days later. During her flight in the boat, she had hidden it in the seam of her pants' waistband. Once she arrived in Quebec, she preferred to work uncountable hours to satisfy our needs rather than sell the diamond that bore witness to her status as wife to my father: Madame Lê Văn An.

I begged Hà and Jacinthe not to tell her about the existence and disappearance of Vincent. She would be shattered to learn that her daughter was living the same fate, the same story, the same abandonment, as herself.

I WENT TO SEE Aline, a long-time friend of Vincent's, who for ten years or so had been running an orphanage at Ước Lệ, about twenty kilometres from Hanoi. This Swiss woman had been a young traveller when one night she'd heard a baby crying in the alleyway behind her little hotel, in the backpackers' neighbourhood. She'd responded to the tears, which had cast a spell on her and kept her in Vietnam ever since. Aline told me that the orphanage received and would continue to receive an automatic and generous contribution from Vincent every month. The money was deposited directly into its account without any formality. She also reminded me that Vincent had often gone off with no return date. I should not be concerned.

I took refuge in the orphanage during all my free time, because there was always a wall to paint, a meal to prepare, a bandage to change, a child to console, a wheelchair to push, a back to rub, a pail to carry, a lullaby to sing. One night, while we were washing the dishes together, Hạnh, a volunteer at the orphanage, recognized my family name. Hạnh adored my father so much that her description seemed to me to be the antithesis of that provided by my brothers, my mother, and all those who had known him. During our second conversation, Hạnh admitted that she'd recognized me because of the photographs of my brothers and myself that covered the walls of my father's room. Some had been sent by Hà, others by my mother.

Hạnh lowered her eyes to hide her tears when she told me that my father had made several attempts to escape, nine in all. Out of pride, he wanted to leave on his own, not sponsored by my mother, and certainly not by my brother Long. To experience the passage was essential to him. He'd first sold everything he possessed to pay for the early voyages. Later, he'd taught English, worked as a waiter in restaurants, and, under a pseudonym, translated a book offered him discreetly by an Australian client. Against all expectations, *The Thorn Birds* became a bestseller, enabling him to try to escape once more. Unfortunately, he'd missed the wave of boat people. Even refugees who had already arrived and settled in camps were being sent back to Vietnam.

My father considered that life was fair in rewarding my mother with our presence and in punishing him with our absence. "He knows you're working in Vietnam," concluded Hạnh. She had the delicacy never again to talk to me about my father. Perhaps she understood that I needed silence in order to hear his voice again, and to find a path back to him.

THE SEASONS jostle each other and return with the same music, except on this first day of spring when Aline, Hạnh, and I can have tea, coatless, at the café near the Lake of the Restored Sword. We are celebrating the admission of one of the orphan children to a neighbourhood school. There are many customers, double the usual number. The easy smiles and spontaneous laughter of the people strolling by give the long lianas of the weeping willows a festive air. But in all the faces around me, I realize that none of them know Vincent. Vincent's Hanoi no longer exists.

I hesitate to announce to Aline and Hạnh the end of my posting in Hanoi. I hesitate to follow my urge to retreat to Nowhere, Oklahoma. I hesitate to escape Vietnam a second time. I hesitate to ask Hạnh for my father's address. I hesitate to leave Vincent's faded sheets, to abandon my hammock weakened from its torn stitching, to throw away the pens whose ink has dried, to take down the mosquito netting, mended every ten centimetres.

I hesitate to leave myself, to abandon the Vi of Vincent.

I hesitate because I intend to leave without saying anything, taking away nothing, except for Vincent's long blue scarf.

As I am hesitating, Hạnh decides for me: "Your father is in Hanoi . . . at the orphanage. He'll be living there for the next month."

"We'll take care of him until he's better," adds Aline.

Before me, the crowd surges towards the other end of the lake. The shell of the hundred-year-old tortoise has just reappeared, bringing good tidings, according to belief.

Born in Saigon in 1968, KIM THÚY left Vietnam with the boat people at the age of ten and settled with her family in Quebec. A graduate in translation and law, she has worked as a seamstress, interpreter, lawyer, restaurant owner, and commentator on radio and television. She lives in Montreal and devotes herself to writing.

SHEILA FISCHMAN is the award-winning translator of some 150 contemporary novels from Quebec. In 2008 she was awarded the Molson Prize in the Arts. She is a Member of the Order of Canada and a chevalier of the Ordre national du Québec. She lives in Montreal.